This Rough
New Land

A NOVEL

by

KENNETH SOLLITT

SUNRISE BOOKS

1707 E Street
Eureka, California 95501

Library of Congress Catalogue Card Number
85-63052

ISBN 0-940652-03-X

DEDICATION

To Maybelle, my devoted wife,
and to our children
Evelyn, Ruth and David.

Grateful acknowledgement is made to Faustina Orner for editorial guidance with this book; and to Thyra Ferre Bjorn, author and friend, whose encouragement has been invaluable and deeply cherished.

ABOUT THE AUTHOR

As a boy growing up on a farm near Sibley, Iowa, (the Stebbinsville of **This Rough New Land)** Kenneth Sollitt was fascinated by stories the old timers told of daring homesteaders moving westward toward opportunity and freedom.

During his young manhood Kenneth spent many hours in the small Sibley Library poring over history books and pioneer novels. One of these, **A Lantern in Her Hand** by Bess Streeter Aldrich, made an impression on him that drew him to writing the stories he had heard as a youth. The first draft of **This Rough New Land** was written in longhand in the Sibley Library. His aunt's journals of her early days on the Iowa prairie helped give the emerging novel focus.

Dr. Sollitt graduated from Sibley High School, Sioux Falls (South Dakota) College, Colgate-Rochester Divinity School and has pastored churches in Vermont, Wisconsin, Illinois, Michigan and New Mexico. He was a script writer for the radio program "Victorious Living" and is a seven time winner of Freedom's Foundation Awards.

Dr. Sollitt and his wife, Maybelle, live in Rio Rancho, New Mexico.

FOREWORD

The gentle breeze played upon the tall prairie grasses giving them the appearance of a great yellow sea. Vast and uninhabited, perhaps even uninhabitable, but inviting in its rich interplay of colors and warmth, who could resist the open prairie in the early days of our country's history? Raw and uncivilized, but open to the taking by any who were stout-hearted and brave and a little stubborn, too.

The men blazed the trails, cleared the land, built houses, fought Indians, and covered their families with protective arms. But when they came home to the warmth of cozy kitchens where there was perhaps a bit of lace on the rough windows, and a bright scrap-calico quilt on the beds, they were reminded that they were not alone in their battle against the harsh elements of the new land. Perhaps the women blazed no trails, fought no Indians, though many were enlisted into these tasks also, but they lent an indomitable courage to this frontier movement that could never be denied. At the very start, they did the most courageous thing thinkable, they gave up everything—comforts, family, security—to follow their men. Such an action at the beginning would prove to be indicative of the manner in which they would continue to tackle the tasks ahead.

Some of these women were shy, retiring, physically weak, while others were buxom, outspoken, hardy. Yet each contributed something no burly frontiersman ever could. They kept the thread of civilization alive in that unchartered prairie. Be it in the simplicity of the fragrance of rising bread or the whir of a spinning wheel. Or more profoundly, in the keeping of the Sabbath or the building of a church or school. The presence of their courageous spirits was a constant reminder of what the new land was all about.

This Rough New Land is the story of such people—the simple, hard-working and brave folk who helped set the tone for the growth of these United States. It chronicles one family which represents many of these qualities. The Bullards are truly real people, folks we could have known, folks who could have been our own ancestors.

There is *Molly Bullard*—everything a pioneer woman had to be to sustain a family through hardships and uncertainty. Her cheerful nature was matched by her soft round face and petite figure. But behind her gentle blue eyes was a woman with enough strength and determination to hold an entire family together. And enough good sense to know her strength came from above.

Her husband, *Sam,* was in many ways typical of the hardy individualists on the western prairie. He was big and strong and exuberant. Everything about him was animated, from his flashing dark eyes to his striking black moustache and booming voice. He hovered over his family with a harsh authority, demanding his own way, not appearing to consider the wishes of any, especially Molly.

The children of such parents would have to be as varied as the snowflakes falling in an Iowa blizzard. Such were the Bullard daughters.

Elsie, the oldest, was the self-appointed boss of the younger three. Her gray-blue eyes presided over a face that was longer than necessary most of the time, for Elsie was an unhappy child. So like her Papa in her self-centered nature, yet at the same time most at odds with him. Thus she tended to see only the gloom in every situation. She was tall and strong and even pretty when she let down her taffy-colored hair and got ready to go someplace where Papa wasn't.

After Elsie, came *Ann.* Her freckled and sunburned round face could not camouflage the serious and sensitive nature reflected in her blue eyes. Straight, chestnut brown hair was usually gathered into long braids and tied with a black or white ribbon. She would always have rather had a red one such as she was given on special occasions, but Mama said, "Black or white fits you best, my solemn one." Yet if she was solemn, she also knew how to enjoy life. She took the hard tasks laid upon her by Papa as something to be expected and so complained less than the others. Sometimes she liked to be alone but this never kept her from making friends and having a good time. Of all the girls, she was most like her Mama.

Vina was everything her older sister, Elsie, was not. Her mischievous dark eyes, which danced like fireflies, and her curly black hair gave her the appearance of the bouncy, exuberant child that she was. Her ready sense of humor and easy-going attitude never failed her. Everyone loved Vina and even more so as she grew older.

Then there was *Lucy,* the tow-headed, blue-eyed baby doll. How could she not be happy with three older sisters to dote upon her and treat her as if she were their own special toy.

And finally baby *Mae,* born during the days of **This Rough New Land,** the newest of the Bullard daughters.

But the Bullards were not alone on the prairie. They touched and were touched by the lives of everyone around them. No one could stand alone in that rough land. The circle of friends and neighbors was almost tantamount to survival itself. Each one seemed to offer a unique quality that enriched the Bullard's lives on the Iowa Prairie.

On the following pages you'll meet and love these neighbors—real pioneers such as Ethan and Hilda Stone, Uncle Phil, Elmer Phillips, Jed Miller—all playing a vital role in the lives of the Bullard family...and all those who helped tame "this rough new land".

The Publishers

PROLOGUE

Among the memories of my boyhood the summers spent with my Aunt Ann in Des Moines remain most vivid and cherished. These seasonal visits began when I was twelve wearing my first pair of long pants, and continued through four unforgettable summers. During those years the pattern of my life was shaped, and the awkward ordeal of growing up made less stumbling and painful because of her wisdom and gentle understanding.

I rarely saw my uncle during these visits. His special studies and professional activities kept him away from the house a good deal, although he usually came home to dinner. This, for a country boy, was a rather formal occasion and never served before eight o'clock in the evening. Perhaps this formality contributed to my considerable awe of him. He was an especially handsome man, and I'm sure was very fond of me. However I was quite content to spend most of those summer days with Aunt Ann.

That first summer stands out clearly in my memory. I had a new suit and a straw hat purchased especially for the occasion. Aunt Ann hadn't seen me since I was three and my mother was anxious that I make a favorable impression. I was nervous, feeling awkward and conspicuous in my new clothes, as the train neared the city.

The train roared into the station, steaming and tooting and screeched to a stop. I picked up my suitcase and stepped out onto the crowded station platform and looked about anxiously. My mother had told me Aunt Ann was past thirty, a venerable age to me. I had pictured her quite differently from the woman I now saw approaching me. This woman looked young and almost girlish in a flowered hat and stylish dress.

She greeted me affectionately but with dignity. She didn't attempt to hug and kiss me as I had feared she might do. Instead she shook my hand and told me what a handsome young man I had become and no wonder my mother was so proud of me. Walking to her carriage, she took my arm and fell into step beside me, talking excitedly about the wonderful summer we were going to have together. I was sure it would be.

But later that afternoon, when we returned from a brief tour of the neighborhood attractions, I wondered if I might not have been hasty in my conclusion. Quite casually Aunt Ann asked me to freshen up and change my clothes, then join her in the library for tea. Great jumping bullfrogs! And as if that weren't enough to spoil things for me she went on to reveal calmly that tea at four o'clock was a daily ritual which she found most relaxing, and it was going to be very pleasant having company for a change.

The excitement that had been building in me since I boarded the train, drained away. I climbed the stairs slowly and took my time about changing my clothes, putting off the stuffy ordeal as long as possible.

But with the tea ritual, as with so many things during the ensuing summers, Aunt Ann surprised me by her innate knowing.

The library, in itself, was a place of quiet wonder. The tea table was spread with a hand-embroidered cloth and set with what I felt sure were her best silver and china. There was a plate of cupcakes with tiny colored candies sprinkled on top, and a silver tray heaped with sandwiches thickly spread with both butter and plum jam. Suddenly my awkwardness fell away and I was as hungry as a growing boy should be. Soon we were talking as easily as if we were having a soda at the ice-cream parlor back home.

Before that first summer was ended I had come to look forward to the daily tea ritual as a time for relaxing after a day of sight-seeing and play. A time also for sharing. I could talk to Aunt Ann about things which interested or troubled me.

She seemed to know what would interest a growing boy who was trying very hard to become a man. She knew instinctively when to indulge the boy, or to provide more serious conversation that would appeal to the budding young man. While I did not comprehend the subtle purpose behind these talks at the time, I now know they, along with the tea ritual, were Aunt Ann's way of teaching me to balance life; to make poise and good manners a source of pride.

Each year, after that first visit, as spring blossomed into summer and school ended, my anticipation began to mount. For months I had been storing up a hundred things to tell Aunt Ann, and as many questions to ask. Perhaps they were trivial and childish, but at the time they seemed exciting and important and she always made me sure that they were.

Sometimes, during those memorable summers, Aunt Ann would tell me about my mother and my other three aunts when they were my age, and the daring things they did together; often in defiance of my strict grandfather and against the wishes of my grandmother who was gentle and understanding but strong-willed. There were also exciting stories about life on the Iowa prairie in the 1880's where my grandfather had taken a homestead; of the long, hard winters and hot summers, of cyclones and prairie fires; and of the work grandfather expected of all of them, not caring that they were girls who yearned for gentler ways.

Listening to these tales I often wondered if they ever had any fun. Once I asked Aunt Ann about that. She smiled and her eyes brightened. Oh, yes, she said . . . and told me about the box-suppers, the dances, the picnics and husking-bees. And buggy rides on balmy summer nights when the sky was thick with stars and crickets chirped all night in the plum-thicket along the roadside; or sleigh-rides across the snow-blanketed prairies.

One thing began to puzzle me. She never talked much about herself. When at last I found the courage to ask her why her answer was quietly evasive. "A lady shouldn't talk about herself, Kenny." And then she smiled. "But I'm keeping a journal. When I'm gone you shall read it and know all about me."

As the years passed I forgot the promised journal, and the memories of those wonderful summers dimmed a little. When I thought of Aunt Ann it was always with deep affection, for to her and to my uncle I owed much that had made my life meaningful. My love of books and music and people. And my decision to become a minister.

Not until Aunt Ann's death a few years ago did I have occasion to recall that long-ago conversation over tea in her library. Among the bequests to various members of the family was a package for me, neatly wrapped and tied with blue ribbon and addressed in her own precise handwriting. It was her journal.

CHAPTER I
1889

We were waiting for Papa to get home from town so we could have supper. Mama, my three sisters and I had waited meals for Papa before but he had never been quite so late as tonight. I knew something was wrong. All evening I'd had that "feeling". Mama called it my sixth-sense, but we never talked about it to anyone else. When you're ten years old life is full of strange new things.

I glanced at Mama sitting by the table with her sewing basket. The lamp-light spilled sunshine over her and I thought as I had a hundred times how beautiful she was. Why couldn't I have been born with light hair instead of chestnut-red? Tonight Mama seemed thoughtful. I wondered if she was getting that "feeling" too. Maybe she was more worried about Papa than that supper was later than usual. But none of us even dreamed that Papa's homecoming that night would change our lives completely.

"Isn't Papa ever coming?" Alvina was seven and always hungry.

Elsie snapped, "You're not the only one that's hungry. Stop making such a fuss!" She was half-way past thirteen and thought she had the right to boss the rest of us. She looked down at four-year-old Lucy playing with her blocks on the floor. "Even Lucy's not complaining."

Alvina's black eyes flashed. She tossed her braids over her shoulder and stuck out her tongue at Elsie. "You think you know everything!"

Elsie jumped up and started toward her. "Mama, Vina's making faces at me again."

Mama went on with her sewing. "Behave yourselves, girls. Papa'll be here any minute now. You'd better get washed up for supper."

"We've been washed for an hour," Elsie grumbled. She grabbed one of Vina's braids and yanked it. Vina let out a yell.

"Elsie! Any more of that and you'll go to bed without supper." Mama seldom spoke harshly to us but she was very strict about discipline.

"Oh, you always let Vina do what she pleases!" Elsie flounced across to the kitchen sink and swished her hands in the granite basin and dried them on the roller towel. Vina waited until she thought it was safe then took her turn at the basin.

I went to the window and peered out. It was too dark to see anything but pretty soon I could hear the sound of the buggy wheels and the dull plop of hooves on the hard dirt road. "Papa's coming! Papa's coming!"

"It's about time," Mama said. She set aside her sewing basket and went to the stove and put in fresh sticks of wood, then pushed a pot of mashed potatoes and the skillet of fried meat she'd been trying to keep warm on the back of the stove, over the fire.

"Elsie, go help Papa with the horses. Vina, put Lucy in her high-chair. Ann, you may dish up the soup now. At least *that's* still hot."

Vina let out a big sigh. "I couldn't have lasted another minute!"

I knew she was just saying that. She knew, as we all did, that no matter how late Papa was we'd never start eating without him.

Elsie came in and went to the wash basin and rinsed her hands again. "Pretty soon there won't be any skin left on 'em," she grumbled to herself.

If Mama heard she didn't let on. Vina asked, "Where's Papa?" Elsie ignored her.

"He'll be here," Mama said. "Hush now, all of you, and take your places at the table." Everyone hushed when Papa was around.

The kitchen door burst open. Papa's huge body filled the doorway. A gust of chilly wind swept through the room making the lamp smoke. He didn't bother to close the door, just stood there a minute. He looked so big and powerful in his blue work shirt and overalls it was no wonder we all feared him. But tonight he seemed different. His eyes looked excited and his mustache quivered like he was going to smile but he didn't.

"Supper ready?" he asked. He didn't seem to know or care

10

how long we had waited supper. He hung his cap and jacket on a hook and went to the table.

"Molly, I've got a great idea," he said, hitching his chair closer.

Mama closed the door and came back to her place at the table "Let's eat, Sam, while things are hot," she said quietly.

Papa looked at her a second like he was going to get mad, then picked up his spoon and tasted the soup. This was our signal to begin eating. We wasted no time.

"Soup needs salt, Molly. Where's the salt?"

"Didn't you bring some from town?"

He brought his fist down on the table so hard our soup splashed onto the clean red-and-white tablecloth. "By golly! I knew I went to Croft's for something. Molly, I've told you a dozen times to write down what you want me to get."

"I only needed one thing, salt."

"One or a dozen, makes no difference. A man has other things on his mind in town besides salt and hairpins and buttons."

"Maybe there's enough in the barrel to fill the shaker once more. I'll see."

"Never mind. I'm not hungry anyway. Here, let me show you something." He took a scrap of newspaper out of his overalls pocket and handed it to her. "Read the part I've marked."

Mama held the paper near the light and read aloud. "The Iowan Land Company controls seventy thousand acres in Osceola County. It is the purpose of this company to bring the land into farm use as soon as possible."

"What does this have to do with us, Sam?"

"I'll tell you what." He pushed his chair back and got up, pacing back and forth. "Seventy thousand acres of the best farm land in the world, all tillable, and they're practically giving it away. Some of it's selling for five dollars an acre. Think of that, Molly! No wonder I forgot the salt. The boys at Croft's were talking about it. Already I've had a good offer for this place. Let's see now . . . ." He sat down again, pushed back his plate and began figuring on the tablecloth. If one of us had done that he'd have threatened to "skin us alive".

11

Mama didn't wait for him to finish. "What do you mean, Sam . . . a good offer for this place?"

Papa went on figuring as if he hadn't heard her. Finally he put down his pencil. "Two thousand clear profit, Molly. And a good farm in Osceola County to boot. You can't beat it!"

"I don't know what you're talking about, Sam. Surely you're not going to trade this place, sight unseen, for land in an Iowa wilderness."

"I didn't say that. I've got *some* sense woman! I'm going out there right away—tomorrow—to look it over. If it's as good as they say it is we'll sell this place and move out there."

Suddenly he noticed his untouched food. "Here, Elsie, warm this up for me. You know how I hate cold food. And Vina, see if you can get a little salt outa that barrel." He turned to Mama. "Better pack my carpet-bag tonight. I want to get an early start. It's a long way to town. We'll have to leave by five to make the 8:10 train."

Mama didn't say anything. Papa had decided. She knew how useless it would be to argue with him now. After a while she went upstairs without finishing her supper. As soon as Papa finished eating he followed her. Elsie and I cleared the table and washed the dishes. Vina undressed Lucy and put her to bed and came back to the kitchen. We whispered among ourselves.

"He can't do it!" Elsie exclaimed. "Mama won't let him," Vina declared.

"She can't stop him and you know it," I whispered.

None of us could believe our home was suddenly threatened. Surely Papa *wouldn't* sell it! But we knew that if he had de-decided to "pull up stakes" and move us to a wilderness with wild Indians and heaven only knew what other dangers, there was nothing any of us could do about it, not even Mama. I thought of the fruit trees we'd planted and watched grow. They would bear fruit next year. And about our house, so nice and comfortable now because of Mama's hard work.

I lay awake a long time that night. It was bad enough for us girls to have to leave our home and friends, but it would break Mama's heart. How could Papa be so mean? Didn't he care how hard moving would be for Mama or that we might all be killed by savages? I wanted to cry. Instead, I

12

hated Papa as hard as I could. And as I thought of what Mama had told us about the years before any of us was born, I hated him even more.

Mama had married Papa in 1874. That spring they left her parents and all their friends in Virginia to find a new home in Illinois. They travelled by covered wagon, with only the food and clothing they needed for the journey. At first, Mama told us, it had been a kind of exciting adventure. Papa had his heart set on pioneering and Illinois, to hear him tell it, was a wonderful place. For weeks the horses plodded on and on and Mama watched the blue mountains and green fields of Virginia fade away. At last they were in southern Illinois. The fields were bigger, the settlements farther apart. She was tired now and frightened, she said, but Papa wanted to push on to the northeast.

"The farther north we go, the better the land. And more of it."

Finally at a small settlement named Minonk, Mama again begged Papa to stop. This time Papa agreed. He bought a small farm and built a cabin.

"We can go on farther north when you feel up to it, Molly," he had told her.

Life was hard in Minonk. There was little civilization and Mama had been used to easier ways. Here, she told us, our little baby brother, Benny, had been born. He had died before he was a year old. The year after he died, Elsie was born. Mama's parents moved from Virginia to Roanoke, Illinois to be near her. Everyone worked hard to build up the little farm, put up a bigger house and add a few more acres of land when crops were good.

Elsie was almost two years old before Papa became restless again. He had a good offer for their farm, he told Mama, and could buy a better one near Saunemin and make a profit besides.

"I tried every way I knew how to make him see it was a mistake," Mama said. "But Papa wouldn't listen. The pasture on the other side of the fence always looked greener to him. He worked hard and thought others should do the same. A quick profit seemed more important to him than comforts."

Mama had packed their things and taken Elsie to Roanoke

13

to Grandma's until Papa built the new house here in Saunemin. I was born in this house while it was still new. Two years later Alvina was born. The house was no longer new when Lucy arrived, but it was comfortable. Last year the barn had been given a fresh coat of paint. The fruit trees were big enough to bear fruit and shade the front porch.

Now Papa was going to "pull up stakes" again and take us away from here to some place a long way off. I went to sleep hating him bitterly.

Mama must have been up most of the night getting Papa's clothes ready. She had washed that day and his shirts had to be ironed. The range was still hot, the flatirons still on the stove, when I came to the kitchen just before daylight. Elsie was putting breakfast on the table. Vina was dressing beside the stove.

"Hurry up, Vina, and fetch the milk from the cellar," Mama said.

"Why can't Ann do it? She's already dressed."

"Because I told you to do it. Ann has to get Lucy up and dressed. Papa will be in for his breakfast pretty soon."

Lucy was dressed and in her high-chair when Papa came in. "It's almost five, Molly. Why isn't breakfast ready? I told you last night we had to leave by five."

"Breakfast *is* ready. We were waiting for you. I'm going to take one of the girls with me for company on the way back."

Mama hadn't mentioned this before. Now all of us begged to be the one taken. Mama considered our pleas as she spooned oatmeal into Papa's bowl.

"It's Ann's turn. She stayed home the last time we went to town. Besides, I want to get her new shoes before the weather gets colder."

Elsie stalked off to the bedroom and slammed the door so hard the dishes rattled. She was wooden-swearing again! Elsie and Papa both did that when they were angry. I thought it was just as wicked to swear that way as with words.

"You'd better fix some sandwiches, Ann. And fill that fruit jar on the cabinet with milk. We'll be late getting back."

Papa spoke through a mouthful of oatmeal. "I don't care which girl you take with you, Molly, but for heaven sake bring home some salt."

14

Mama put on her coat and wrapped a fascinator about her head while she gave last-minute instructions. Vina was to look after Lucy, wash the dishes and tidy up the house. Elsie was to take the cows to pasture and go ahead with digging the root-crops. "And both of you behave yourselves. No quarreling, mind you!"

"We won't have time to fight," Vina said with a grin.

It was still dark when we climbed into the springwagon. I settled myself between Mama and Papa on the hard seat, softened a little by an old quilt spread over it. Mama tucked the laprobe about our legs and feet. September mornings now held a nip of frost.

All the way to town Papa talked about wonderful Osceola county and the land he was going to buy, and how much better off we'd be in Iowa where "a man could stretch and grow with the country". Mama didn't say much. I thought about the farm we had now and couldn't see how one in Iowa would be better. We had a creek in our pasture and a big barn with a haymow where we played when it rained. There was a swing in the elm tree behind the house where we played when the sun was hot. I almost cried when I thought about giving up the nice bedroom Elsie and Vina and I shared. Only last summer Mama had made the prettiest yellow and white curtains for us and finished the patch-quilt she'd been making in her spare time. How could Papa *want* to change anything? Once Mama said Papa had "roaming fever". I guess he did. He always wanted to be going somewhere else. Any place seemed too crowded for him by the time it got settled enough to be comfortable.

It was sun-up when we reached Saunemin. My legs were stiff from sitting so long. Papa got his carpet-bag from the back of the springwagon and he and Mama went inside. I stayed outside and ran up and down the station platform to keep warm. Just being in town to see the train come in was exciting. Presently it came, panting and puffing, and groaned to a screeching stop. The engine snorted like an iron monster, breathing fire and smoke. The five coaches looked pretty dirty but Papa wouldn't mind that. He'd soon be on his way to a new place called Osceola County.

Papa kissed Mama goodbye and told me to be a good girl,

15

and climbed aboard. We watched the big engine heave and snort belching a cloud of black smoke. It was so thick we couldn't see whether Papa was waving goodbye or not. We stood a while on the platform in the cold morning wind until the train became a tiny speck in the distance. I looked at the silvery tracks glistening in the morning light and wondered how anything so small could hold up that big monster engine all the way to Iowa.

Mama took my hand and we hurried along the wooden sidewalk to Croft's store.

"Don't forget the salt," I reminded her as Mr. Croft wrapped my new shoes in brown paper. They were the prettiest black high-button shoes I had ever owned.

When we got back to the hitching post where the horses were tied Mama stood beside the wagon for a while after she helped me up. I could tell she had something on her mind. Maybe she was hoping what I was. That Papa would *stay* in Osceola County and let us stay in Saunemin. Pretty soon she picked up her skirts and climbed up beside me and slapped the reins against the mare's flanks.

"Ged-up, old girl," she said, sounding angry. "We have to do the work while the stallion gallops off to greener pastures!"

It was a funny thing for her to say. Why, she'd the same as called Papa a stallion! I smiled to myself at the thought. The way Papa pranced and snorted when he got excited or angry *was* just like our stallion behaved sometimes. But I knew Mama loved him. I guess we all did. Most of the time, though, we were too afraid of him to love him. I supposed he loved us too. Mama said he did. But he never showed it the way Mama did. He was always ordering us about. His word was law and we obeyed. Even Mama most of the time. But sometimes she'd "put her foot down" when she thought we children weren't listening. Once I'd heard her talking with Uncle Phil about Papa's temper. "He's a lot like one of those steam-engines," she said. "Has to blow off steam now and then to get started again." Maybe, I thought, Papa was more like an engine than a stallion. Engines were always going to some other place.

"You must be getting hungry," Mama said. "We'll stop under the next tree and have our sandwiches and milk."

16

It was almost dark when we got home. Elsie and Vina met us at the gate with a dozen questions. Was Papa really going to sell the farm and take us to Iowa? Where was Iowa, anyway? What kind of place was it? If Papa liked it so much why couldn't he go there and let us stay here?

Mama hurried us inside out of the cold. All she said was, "We'll see." She went upstairs to change her clothes. When she came down Elsie brought her a cup of coffee. "As soon as we get the chores done I'll see about supper."

Everyone worked hard when Papa was around. Now there would be more work for all of us. Was that what Mama was talking about when she called Papa a stallion?

A week passed. We went about our daily chores uneasily awaiting Papa's return. Each day made the waiting harder. Maybe he *had* decided to stay in Iowa without us! The thought was comforting. Another week went by. One night while we were eating supper there were suddenly footsteps on the porch.

"He's back!" I cried and ran to open the door.

But it wasn't Papa. It was Uncle Phil. He wasn't really our uncle, we just called him that. His name was Robert Phillips but everyone called him Phil, even Mama and Papa. He lived on the farm next to ours.

"Come in, Phil," Mama called. "You must have smelled those apple pies I baked today."

He laughed. "I sure do now. And the coffee smells almost as good. It's nippy out tonight."

He finished the pie and coffee before he said, "I got a letter from Sam today, Molly. I guess he figured I'd get in for the mail sooner than you would." He took the letter from his pocket and handed it to Mama.

She looked at the envelope first. "It's postmarked Stebbensville, Iowa. Where is that?"

"In Osceola County. The letter tells all about it."

Mama unfolded the letter slowly and read it aloud.

Osceola, Papa wrote, was a famous Indian chief known for his brave and savage fighting. The county had been named for him. Stebbinsville was a thriving new town named after Colonel Josiah Stebbins, one of the first white settlers in the county and also a famous Indian fighter. The first house in Stebbinsville had been built in 1871, but now with the Sioux

17

City and St. Paul railroad the town was booming. Houses were springing up like corn after a spring rain. A courthouse and school were under construction. Already the town had its own weekly newspaper.

Mama looked up at Uncle Phil who was cleaning his pipe over the wood box. "He talks about Stebbinsville as if *he* had built it."

Uncle Phil grinned. "I guess you *could* say he seems pretty sold on the place, all right." He blew on the stem of his pipe. "I'm always interested in good land at a cheap price, but I'm a mite too old to start acting like Daniel Boone."

"And so is Sam. By the way, Phil, do you know who made him an offer for this place?

"Sure do." He lighted his pipe slowly. "I did."

"I'll declare, Phil, you've got a lot more sense than he has."

Uncle Phil drew on his pipe and sent up a wispy cloud of smoke. "I don't think Sam would agree. Still, I thought it might be a good idea to keep the place in friendly hands just in case you wanted to come back sometime." He sighed. "I'm sure going to miss you folks, Molly. *And* your apple pie," he added, grinning.

"Don't be so sure we're going. We haven't gone yet." She handed him the letter.

"Keep it. You may want to read it over again." He put on his cap and went out.

When I went to bed that night I kept thinking about what Mama had said, that we hadn't gone yet. Did she really mean we might not go at all? Oh, I hoped so. But I knew it was useless to hope. The way Papa wrote about Iowa he was determined to move all of us out there. And when Papa was that determined not even Mama could stop him.

A few days later when we were finishing supper, we heard a wagon stop at our gate and Papa's booming voice. "Thanks, Phil, 'til you're better paid."

Papa dropped his carpet-bag inside the door and hugged Mama. She took his coat and hung it up, brought him a cup of coffee. "The stew's still hot, Sam. You must be starved."

"A piece of that pie will do. I did it, Molly! Bought a quarter section from the Iowan Land Company. We have to take possession no later than March first. Wait 'til you see it!

It's the richest soil I ever saw. Much better than we have here. Our place is only five miles from town and every inch of it good farm land. Why, it's so level you can see for miles. Miles and miles of prairie grass this high . . ." He drew a line across his hip with the side of his hand.

Papa should have been tired from his long trip but he didn't seem to be. He pranced about the kitchen talking about Iowa. I couldn't help thinking about what Mama had said. She went right on setting the bread she would bake tomorrow and putting the beans to soak. She kept her back to him. I knew she was crying. Papa was too busy prancing to notice.

"Gee, Papa," Vina said, forgetting she wasn't supposed to use that word, "With grass *that* high Lucy could get lost right in the front yard."

Papa grabbed Lucy and tossed her in the air, caught her and hugged her close. "We sure don't want to lose our little pigeon, do we?"

"How are the roads, Sam?" Mama asked without looking up.

"Roads?" He put Lucy down. "Of course there's no roads yet, not to speak of. But there's plenty of place to put them. The whole country's been measured off in sections a mile square. In no time at all there'll be roads criss-crossing those prairies like a checkerboard. But in winter nobody needs to worry about roads. The snow gets so deep and hard you can strike off across the prairie in a bobsled, right over fences and everything . . . when there are fences. Most people don't have 'em yet."

Suddenly I thought about the trip Mama had made from Virginia to Illinois in a covered wagon when there were no roads, and the baby brother who died that winter. Was Iowa like that? And if Mama got sick how would we get a doctor?

"But the snow will be gone by April," Mama was saying. "Then what, Sam? Mud?"

"Spring plowing and planting in the richest black loam in the world, that's what." His voice boomed with excitement. It was long past Lucy's bedtime and ours but he went right on talking about the wonders of Iowa and Stebbinsville.

After a while he stood up and stretched and threw out his arms. "I tell you, Molly, all roads will soon lead to Iowa It's going to be the center of a great new world!"

19

Mama covered the bread pan with a clean white cloth and sat down. Papa was too excited to notice how sad she looked. He sat down again and began drawing on the tablecloth. "Here's Stebbinsville. See? And here's Sioux Falls. There's an overland freight route between the two by way of a little settlement called Rock Rapids."

Elsie and Vina looked over his shoulder following the imaginary road. Lucy climbed into Mama's lap and went to sleep. I closed my eyes tight and refused to look. But Papa's voice was too loud to be shut out. He was talking about the settlers now. ". . . like this man Bancroft I met. A real pioneer. Do you know what he did? In August of 1872 he drove all the way from Stebbinsville to Cherokee, more than fifty miles, with an ox team and covered wagon to meet his wife and four children. And during the whole trip, he said, he saw nothing but prairie grass and marshes. Not a single tree."

Mama stared at him. "No trees, Sam? Not even one?"

"That's right, Molly. Every inch of that land is tillable."

I wondered what they built houses out of in Iowa if there were no trees for lumber. But I knew better than to interrupt Papa. Pretty soon he answered my silent question.

". . . . the Bancrofts were soon settled in a little sod house that later became the first school in the township."

A sod house! Sod, I knew, was just dirt held together by grass roots. How could anyone, except maybe a prairie dog or badger, build a house fit to live in out of dirt? I looked at the sturdy walls of our kitchen and the smooth white board floor Mama kept scrubbed so clean you could almost "eat off it"; and the big cupboard filled with her pretty dishes, the wide window with blue-checked gingham curtains, and the big iron stove that kept the room cozy and warm all winter. What would it be like to live in a sod hut and maybe go to school in another sod hut? Maybe there wouldn't even be a school. It was all too horrible to think about.

". . . . and that fall Mr. Bancroft's woman gave birth in that sod house to the first white baby girl in the township."

Vina's curiosity got the best of her again. "What color were the other babies, Papa?"

Papa didn't answer. Maybe he didn't hear her. He was lost in an Iowa blizzard.

". . . . the worst blizzard in Iowa history was about to hit those prairies, but of course Bancroft didn't know that then. They were low on firewood so he hitched his team to the bobsled and headed for Big Ocheyedan Creek several miles away where some willows grew. He had the sled half loaded when the storm struck. Before he could say Jack Robinson the whole load was blown clean off the bobsled. Bancroft held onto the sled and tied the lines behind his back and let the wind take them. All day they wandered through that storm. Late that night the team stopped. Bancroft could see a light ahead. He shouted for help. After a while a man struggled toward him holding a lantern in a milkpail to keep it from blowing out. He got Bancroft into his sod shanty and left him to thaw out while he took care of the team. Then he fed Bancroft salt pork and mush and they talked. Do you know, Molly, that wind had blown Bancroft thirty miles from home!"

"How long do these storms last?"

"That one lasted four days and nights."

"I was just wondering how Mrs. Bancroft and the children got along without fuel all that time."

Papa looked surprised. "Gosh, Molly. I didn't think to ask Bancroft."

Elsie asked the question that was in my mind. "Did you stay in a sod house, Papa, in Stebbinsville?"

"Goodness, no, child. Stebbinsville's come a long way since 1872. It's the prettiest little town you ever saw now. I stayed in a boarding house built just before the railroad came through. They had to haul the lumber from Minnesota over fifty miles away. And those hardy pioneers hauled enough lumber by ox-cart to build a two-story frame building." Suddenly he slapped his knee and laughed. "And do you know what? They were in such a hurry to finish it before the railroad workers arrived, they plum' forgot to put in a stairway!"

Elsie gasped, "But how could they . . . .?"

". . . get to the second floor? They just nailed cleats to the outside of the building and let the roomers climb up."

"Sam, tall tales are for grownups, not children."

"It's God's truth, Molly. Bruckner told me himself. He owns the store there. Musta been kind of embarrassing for women with hoopskirts, eh, Molly!"

Mama smiled and got up. Lucy still slept in her arms. "Now that we've all come through the blizzard safely I think it's time we went to bed . . . by an inside stairway. It's almost midnight."

We'd never been allowed to stay up so late. Any other night we'd have been sent to bed by nine o'clock.

Long after the lamps were out Elsie, Vina and I lay awake whispering about the strange place Papa was going to take us to. Vina thought it might be a wonderful adventure. Elsie and I shared Mama's fears. How could it be anything *but* awful with sod houses and no roads and not even one tree? In the next room I could hear Mama and Papa still talking in low voices after Vina and Elsie were asleep. I prayed with all my heart that Mama would refuse to go. But I knew how stubborn Papa was, and that Mama was often too gentle to oppose him.

When finally I fell asleep I dreamed I was a prairie dog living all winter in a hole in the ground, and when spring came I was a furry mass of skin and bones, too weak to move. So I was left to roast to death on a treeless prairie. I must have cried out. I awoke to find Mama standing by my bed. She sat down beside me and smoothed my forehead gently.

"It was only a bad dream, dear. Everything is going to be all right. Jesus will be with us wherever we have to go." She tucked the covers about my shoulders and kissed my cheek, and tiptoed out.

CHAPTER II
1890

We had real nice neighbors. They were more neighborly than ever that winter. Someone was always dropping in or stopping by on their way back from town. Papa was sure they came to hear him tell about Iowa. His stories got bigger and bigger each time he told them. But I didn't think they were very interested in the wonders of Iowa. I think they came as often as they could to see us because soon they would never see us again.

Uncle Phil came often. As the new owner of the farm he and Papa had a lot to talk about. What they talked about, though, didn't seem very important. I think he came because he dreaded to see us leave.

One night when Papa was smelling up the kitchen oiling and mending his harness by the stove, Uncle Phil stopped in. He sat by the kitchen table smoking his pipe and listening to Papa's big plans about Iowa. I noticed he kept glancing at Mama in the big rocker knitting a fresh supply of stockings for us girls. When he could get a word in, he said, "I think I'll put a gate in the far fence of that north forty, Sam. Sorta tie the two farms together."

"Makes good sense. No use hauling hay and grain clear around by the road now you own both farms."

"It's a big place for me and the boys to handle. They're going to be good farmers, though. They do fine now for boys their age." He sighed. "Hard to realize Elmer'll be sixteen come spring, and Freddie's going on fourteen. I've done my best to see they're boys Stella'd be proud of. Seems only yesterday she was wearing herself out trying to keep 'em outa mischief."

"They're fine, healthy boys, Phil. And there's nothing better than hard work to turn boys into responsible men. Or girls into women, I guess."

There was a long silence. Uncle Phil said, "It's going to be mighty lonesome around here without you folks. I sure hate to see you go."

Mama looked up and smiled. Papa went on oiling the harness.

The dreaded day finally came. A day we would long remember. The sun broke through the clouds that February morning for the first time in weeks. The wind was cold and the fields were covered with deep snow. Uncle Phil came over to help crate the furniture and load it onto the wagons. It would be shipped by freight to Iowa. Papa was rushing about pounding nails, moving boxes, giving orders, and yelling at us girls.

"Alvina, I told you to keep outa my way," he shouted when she tried to help. Before she could move he yelled again. "Get that stuff outa the table drawer. What's the matter with you? Always under foot when I'm busy and never around when I need you."

He talked the same way to Elsie and me. And sometimes to Mama. Once Elsie talked back. He put down the hammer and turned her over the packing box and gave her several hard whacks. Elsie didn't cry but the look she gave Papa was awful. I quickly followed Mama upstairs. Papa's angry voice called after us.

"Molly! Dog-gone it, where are you? Bring the chairs from the bedrooms."

Uncle Phil said, "I'll get 'em, Sam. You shouldn't ask Molly to lift things in her condition. That's why Stella isn't with me now, lifting things she shouldn't."

"Whose woman is she anyway?" Papa snapped.

Uncle Phil didn't answer, but he came upstairs and carried the chairs down. I wondered what he meant by "her condition." Mama seemed well and strong. A few times, though, when Papa was away she'd been kinda sick in the mornings. But anyone could see she was gaining weight so she must be all right.

At last all the furniture was crated and loaded onto Uncle Phil's wagon. He and Elmer would take it to the station for shipping. He had brought a bed from his place for Mama and Papa to use our last night in the house. We girls would make a bed of blankets on the floor.

Mama awakened us early the next morning. "Up now, all of you. Breakfast is ready. I've let you sleep as late as possible."

Breakfast was bacon and eggs and fried potatoes served from the frying pan into our plates. We ate standing up. The bedding and cooking utensils were then loaded into our wagon with the trunks and suitcases. Bundled against the cold we waited for Mama. She went through the house pulling down all the shades. Lucy started to cry.

"Don't be a crybaby," Elsie scolded. But she picked Lucy up and carried her outside. Vina and I followed. She was wiping her eyes. I wanted to cry but it wouldn't help. I whispered to Lucy, "Don't cry, pigeon. We're going to Roanoke to see Grandma and Grandpa."

Pretty soon Mama came out and slowly closed the door.

Papa was already in the wagon calling to us to "get a move on." Mama lifted Lucy onto the seat beside him, and climbed up. Elsie, Vina and I scrambled into the back. We made a nest in the straw among trunks and suitcases and covered ourselves with a thick horseblanket. Elsie had the best spot behind the biggest trunk out of the wind. Uncle Phil came from the barn. Papa issued final orders as if he still owned the place.

"Better watch that thistle patch on the east forty, Phil. The girls hoed it last fall but they probably didn't get all of 'em. You know how kids do things."

"It takes years to get rid of a thistle patch, Sam. The girls did a good job. I hope my boys do as well."

"Well, you can worry about that now. We're off to a big new country." He slapped the lines.

"I hope it's also a good country, Sam. Take care of Molly and the girls." He reached a hand up to Mama. "Goodby, Molly. Danged if I don't wish I was goin' with you!"

Papa called goodbye and yelled "ged-up" to the team. We were on our way. As soon as we were out of Uncle Phil's hearing Papa said sharply, "What did he mean by that?"

Mama didn't answer, but she turned and looked back as we were doing. Uncle Phil was standing in the driveway smoking his pipe and waving.

"Maybe it's a good thing I'm getting you away from here, Molly. What's been going on between you two?"

"That's a foolish question and you know it, Sam. Phil's the best friend we'll ever have." After a while she said, "I didn't realize how much our house needed painting."

"It's not our house now. Phil can paint it if he wants to."

After that there was silence except when the wagon wheels

rattled over bumpy frozen ground and crusted snowdrifts. February was still too cold to feel like spring, especially this early in the morning. I snuggled deeper into my straw bed. The sun got redder and climbed higher. Its rays reached down into the wagon box like long fingers, warming us. The rhythm of horses' hooves on the frozen road and the steady rumble of the wagon made me sleepy. As I drifted off the hoof-beats seemed to be saying, "Going to Grandma's. Going to Grandma's!"

When I awakened the sun was high above us. The horses were trotting, and Mama and Papa were bouncing and swaying on the spring seat exactly as they had been doing before I fell asleep. Lucy slept in Mama's arms. Vina leaned against the wagon box, her head back and her eyes closed. She winced every time the wagon went over a bump and banged her head where the braids were rolled up under her winter hood. Elsie had called Lucy a crybaby. Now she lay on her stomach in the straw and dabbed her eyes with a mittened hand.

Looking over the endgate I saw that the houses were getting closer together. We were coming into a town. The horses slowed to a walk finally and Papa called, "Whoa! Time for dinner." He climbed down and took Lucy. Mama climbed down by herself. We crawled out over the endgate, glad to stretch our legs.

"Where are we?" I asked.

"Can't you read?" Elsie waved a mittened hand toward a sign over the door of a nearby building. *The Pontiac — Board and Room by Day or Week.*

"Are we almost there?" Vina asked.

"We've come twelve miles," Mama told us. "We have twice that far to go before we get to Minonk where Elsie was born. We'll stay there overnight and go on to Grandma's tomorrow."

Minonk, I knew, was where Benny was buried. Mama didn't mention that.

"We'll *never* get there," Elsie complained. "How can we go twice as far this afternoon as we've come this morning?"

"It isn't noon yet, dear. But this is the last place to eat before we get to Minonk."

"Twenty-four miles between towns!" Elsie grumbled. "If the towns are any farther apart in Iowa I hope I never live to see the old place!"

"Don't say that, Elsie!" Alvina cried.

"She doesn't mean that at all," Mama said. "We're all tired and hungry. Come along."

Papa unhitched the horses and led them around to the big livery stable in back of the rooming house. We went up onto the big front porch out of the wind to wait for Papa.

We were too early for dinner the woman in charge told us when Papa made his demands. We could either wait an hour in the Boarders' parlor, she said, or we could have whatever she could fix in a hurry. I expected Papa to get mad but he didn't. "Bring us whatever you have. We're in a hurry. Got a long way to go before nightfall," he said politely.

We had more bacon and eggs and fried potatoes. Soon we were on our way again.

Never was there a day like this one! It seemed to go on forever. At last the sun went down. Chilly air drifted into the wagon-bed. Finally Papa stopped long enough to let Mama and Lucy climb down into the wagon-bed with the rest of us. We were hungry and tired and cold and there were still eight miles to go before we reached Minonk.

As night fell I thought of the awful darkness that had filled the house early this morning when Mama drew the shades. After a while the moon came up. It looked like a cold buckwheat pancake. Slowly it rose above the endgate getting smaller as it climbed. Pretty as it was it brought no warmth or comfort to us. The misery and fear and cold seemed to get worse with every turn of the wagon wheels. Mama tried to soften our terrors by singing hymns and hugging us close to her.

It seemed a long time before the horses turned into a driveway and stopped beside a farm house. A man came out, holding up a lighted lantern. As its glow fell on Papa's face the man exclaimed, "Well, Sam Bullard! Why didn't you let us know you was comin'? Climb down and come inside. Supper's over but the missus can fix you some bacon and eggs in a jiffy."

He looked a little surprised when he saw Papa was not alone. But it didn't seem to make any difference. His wife welcomed us with a big smile and showed us into the front room while she fixed us a big platter of fried bacon and eggs and potatoes. We were so hungry by this time no one minded eating them for the third time today.

I slept snug as a kitten that night. Elsie awakened me the next morning complaining she hadn't slept a wink.

"You sure snored loud awake," Vina teased.

"How do you know?" I asked her. We all laughed.

It took me a little while to realize where we were. When I did remember I closed my eyes trying not to. Maybe if I kept them closed the awful feeling of loneliness and loss would go away. Lucy stirred beside me. "Where's Mama?"

Elsie answered her. "Downstairs helping with breakfast, I suppose. You kids better get up if you want any."

I crawled out of our nice warm bed and shivered into my clothes, then helped Lucy. Fluffy new snow had fallen during the night but the sun was coming up red and warm looking. "How much farther is it to Grandma's?" I asked.

"Too far if you ask me!" Elsie snapped. "Last night Papa said it was about fifteen miles."

"That's not so far," Vina said, and jumped out of bed and scrambled into her clothes. Her eyes sparkled as she combed her long hair.

"I don't know what you're so cheerful about," Elsie scolded.

"Because we're going to Grandma's and it's only fifteen more miles." Vina always seemed to look on the bright side of things. New places excited her. In that way she was a little like Papa.

"And after that, Iowa! You won't feel so cheery when you're wading snow-drifts up to your neck."

Vina went on braiding her hair. "Oh, I don't know about that. Just think of all the snowmen we can make."

"You make me tired!" Elsie said. She turned her back and went to the window.

I felt sorry for her in a way. Most of the time she had good reason to grumble. Being the oldest, Papa made her work harder than the rest of us. I suppose she was thinking about how much more work there would be to do in Iowa.

When everyone was dressed we went downstairs. At the bottom of the stairs we stopped and looked about for Mama. She was nowhere in sight. Papa was in the front room talking to the man who had welcomed us last night. "It's a great country, Seward," he boasted. "Good soil and lots of space. Makes a man feel ten feet tall."

28

Mrs. Seward, a large motherly woman, came into the dining room with a platter of pancakes. "Breakfast's ready, folks. Come eat while the cakes is hot."

Papa and Mr. Seward came but not Mama. Papa didn't seem to notice she wasn't here. Not until Mrs. Seward came from the kitchen with a pot of steaming coffee. "Where's Molly? She isn't sick is she?" Papa looked up from his plate, puzzled. "I thought she was helping you in the kitchen." He got up and went to the foot of the stairs and called, "Molly! Breakfast's ready."

"She's not upstairs, Papa," I said.

"Then where the devil is she? Did she say anything to you kids?"

"She was gone when we woke up," Elsie told him.

Mrs. Seward sounded worried. "Are you sure she ain't sick, Sam? In her condition . . ."

Breakfast was forgotten. Mrs. Seward began to search the house. The men grabbed their jackets and headed for the barn. "Though I don't see what she'd be doing out there this time of the morning," Papa grumbled. But he sounded worried too.

"Did your mother seem very upset about leaving Saunemin?" Mrs. Seward asked us when the men were gone.

"No more upset than the rest of us," Elsie told her.

"But she *was* pretty upset," Vina added. I swallowed hard. Elsie hadn't seen Mama crying, and I didn't know Vina had until now.

All of us huddled close to the window looking toward the barnyard. Lucy began to whimper. "I want Mama!"

Papa came back in a few minutes. "No sign of her anywhere."

"Thank goodness!" Mrs. Seward exclaimed. I knew then what she had feared.

A minute later she said, "We're all actin' like fools. Molly ain't in the house or the barn, so she's got to be outdoors somewhere. It snowed last night. All we have to do is look for her tracks."

Papa and Mr. Seward hurried out.

"You girls sit down now and eat them pancakes 'fore they're stone cold. We'll find your mama, don't you worry!"

We tried to eat to please her, but no one was hungry. Papa

29

came back in a few minutes. "There's tracks down the lane and up the road to the north. Looks like she decided to walk to town. But what on earth for?"

I left the table and went to the window. From here I could see down the lane to the main road. Surely Mama wouldn't just go away and leave all of us! But why had she gone, and where? We had to find her! We couldn't go to Iowa without her. I looked down the lane again. Mama was turning into it from the road.

"There's Mama! She's all right!" I cried. The others crowded about the window.

"She'd better have a good excuse for this behavior," Papa said, his face red with anger.

"Don't be too hard on her, Sam. Women get strange notions at a time like this," Mrs. Seward said. "Now back to the table, all of you. I'll bring some fresh cakes. Best we don't act concerned about her."

We heard the kitchen door open. I put my hand on Lucy's knee to keep her from running to meet Mama.

"Breakfast's ready, Molly," Mrs. Seward said as calmly as if nothing had happened.

"Were you waiting for me?"

"Like one pig waits for another!" Mrs. Seward laughed.

"I took a little walk over to the cemetery."

"Lan' sakes, Molly! You shouldn't a gone that far on a morning like this in your condition."

Mama smiled. I wondered again what they meant by "your condition." Mrs. Seward had said that a couple of times since we got here, and Uncle Phil had said the same thing.

"It *was* farther than I remembered. But I was afraid Sam wouldn't have time to drive over there and I wanted to see Benny's grave once more. Where we're going is a long way from Minonk."

Papa didn't say anything. Mr. Seward put his hand on Papa's arm. "Best to make allowances at times like this." In a louder tone he said, "Eat hearty, folks. Likely be quite a spell 'fore you stick your feet under our table again."

Papa kept his eyes on his plate until he'd finished three more pancakes. He spoke then without looking at Mama. "Is Benny's grave being cared for all right?"

30

"Yes, Sam. Real well."

"He was our first born, a son," Papa explained. "I sure hope the next one's a boy."

"And that he lives," Mama added softly.

Most of the new snow was gone by noon when we reached Roanoke. Papa drove slowly through the town and turned into Elm Street where Grandma and Grandpa lived. Elsie and Vina and I forgot how tired and cold we were. We leaned over the side of the wagon eager for our first glimpse of the white picket fence and white frame house with its big porch. Suddenly there it was! And Grandma and Grandpa were hurrying down the front steps to greet us.

Grandma's kitchen was big and warm. There were white ruffled curtains at the windows and red geraniums in clay pots on the sills. The nickel-trimmed range shone like a black mirror. Good smells came from steaming granite kettles and a bubbling coffee pot. Grandpa took our wraps. Grandma was busy at the stove.

"Everything's ready," she said cheerily, and I knew how glad she was to see us. "Sit right down, all of you. You must be starved after your long trip."

Papa spoke up. "I'll eat anything but bacon and eggs and fried potatoes, by golly!" He explained why and everyone had a good laugh.

Mama was a good cook but somehow food always tasted different at Grandma's table. Maybe it was because we didn't have to wait for Papa to start eating before we could. As soon as Grandpa said "grace" it was all right to start. And Grandma always gave us second helpings without our asking for them.

After lunch, before Papa could begin talking about Iowa, I asked Grandma if we could go in the parlor and look at the stereoscope pictures. She said we could but it might be chilly in there today. "Charles" — that's what she called Grandpa — "will you make a fire in the base-burner?"

The parlor in Grandma's house was a place of wonder and beautiful things. There were ecru lace curtains at two large bay windows facing the street. The hooked rug Grandma had made herself, was like a floor of red roses. There was a big couch covered with soft green velvet, and a platform-rocker to match. Just being close to these pretty things made you feel good all

31

over. As soon as the room was warm enough Grandma shooed all of us into the parlor. Elsie brought the stereoscope and pictures from the black walnut table where they were kept. It had a marble top and stood in the center of the room. We sat in a row on the couch awaiting our turn with the magic box. How could looking at pictures through that thing make them seem so *real?*

Papa sat in the platform rocker. Grandpa insisted Mama take the other rocker. He and Grandma sat on the carved walnut chairs with horse-hair seats. They looked uncomfortable to me but I guess they weren't. Mama and Grandma were talking a blue streak and Papa wasn't saying anything for a change. I noticed Mama kept looking at the piano. She loved Grandma's parlor, especially that lovely black mahogany piano. It had a green velvet runner on top with gold tassels all around it.

"I hope the girls can have a parlor and a piano some day," I heard her say when I was waiting my turn with the pictures. "Iowa seems so far away from such things I'm afraid it will be a long time."

Papa didn't hear her, I guess. He'd been silent as long as he could and now was telling Grandpa all about the wonders of Iowa.

We finished looking at all the stereoscope pictures finally and put the slides carefully into their special box. Elsie put it back on the table beside the china lamp with its hand-painted globe. Now was the time for Grandma to bring out the second wonder — her red plush-covered photograph album. She didn't forget! It was kept on the shelf of a gilded metal stand. On top of the stand was a big fern plant in a silver pot. The surprising thing about the album was not just the pictures. When you turned the last thick page a tiny music box, hidden in the back, played *Should Old Acquaintance Be Forgot.*

We put the album on the floor and squatted around it pretending to be surprised when we came to Grandpa's picture. It was the last one in the album and we knew the music box was next. We turned the pages again and again waiting with excitement for the first tinkling sound.

Grandpa was a kind man but very stern and proper. He wore a full black beard and sideburns which made him look exactly like the last picture in the album. Elsie said he used whisker dye but we didn't believe her. Even if he did, we loved him anyway. But you could never tell what he was thinking so we were careful to remember our manners when he was around and not giggle too much.

Supper in Grandma's house was called dinner. When she called to us from the kitchen that dinner was ready, we put the album in its place on the stand, straightened our clothes and went to the kitchen to wash our hands at the sink, then marched into the dining room. Meals at Grandma's table brought out our best manners. We sat up straight in our chairs, and while we waited for the others to sit down, admired the beautiful room. The furniture was all golden oak and it looked like gold because it was so shiny. The sideboard had several little drawers and diamond-shaped mirrors between the small shelves above the polished top where Gandma kept her silver service. It also had glass balls covered with metal on each leg. Grandma called these "lion's claws". The dining table was really round but tonight Grandma had added a "leaf" to make it big enough for all of us. She put on her best white damask tablecloth and was using her fancy dishes and best silverware. Grandma always made us feel like we were very important. Everyone, including Mama and Grandma, wore their best clothes.

Grandpa stood behind his chair at the head of the table. When Grandma and Mama were ready to sit down he held their chairs for them, then took his place. Papa stood at the other end of the table, waiting for the ladies to be seated. With both the base-burner and the kitchen range going at the same time, the room had become very warm so before Papa sat down he took off his coat and hung it on the hall rack beside Grandpa's silk hat.

I glanced at Grandpa who was waiting to say "grace". He was dressed to perfection and looked exactly like the last picture in the album. His handsome beard covered almost all of his shirt front—all that showed above his fancy vest. And now he was staring at Papa as though he had come to the table in his underwear. Presently he bowed his head and said "grace" in his usual manner, but ended with a special plea.

"Great Jehovah, be pleased to remind Sam Bullard before the next meal that he *is* a Southern gentleman. Amen."

33

Everyone looked at Papa except Grandpa. He went right ahead carving the roast. Papa's face got redder and redder. I thought he was going to explode like a fire-cracker. Grandma filled the water glasses from a cut-glass pitcher and said nothing. Mama and the rest of us stared at our plates and waited for the storm. After a brief silence it came.

"Molly, get me my coat!" Papa demanded in a loud voice.

Mama quickly did as he asked. Papa stood up and put it on and looked down the table at Grandpa. "When a Bullard wants something, Mr. Dauber, he says so right out. *He* doesn't go whining to the Lord about it!"

Grandpa went on carving. "You'd best keep on speaking terms with the Lord, Sam. He's been mighty generous with you, giving you Molly Dauber for a wife."

This was too much for Papa. "Bring me my hat, Molly! No, never mind I'll get it myself." He stalked into the hall, grabbed his hat and clapped it on his head and went out. He slammed the door so hard I knew he was wooden-swearing something awful. We sat very still and didn't say anything. Grandpa served the roast and browned potatoes and passed our plates to us. Mama passed the biscuits, Grandma her pretty flowered-china gravy-boat. Elsie reached for the pickle-caster. It was made of cut-glass with a silver base and had a fancy silver handle. On the side was a tiny glass hook for the pickle-fork, and the cover had a little silver cucumber knob.

I looked around the table wondering if it was all right to start eating. Everyone seemed disturbed but Grandpa. He finished serving and picked up his knife and fork. "Looks mighty good. Sam's going to be sorry he lost his temper before he got a taste of this." He glanced at Mama. "But I like his spunk. He's a real Southerner though, Molly, even if he does forget his manners at times. He doesn't take anything from anybody. But how long is he going to have to farm before he learns it's the empty wagon that makes the most noise?"

Grandma added, "Yes, he's a fine man. We're all proud of Sam, Molly."

Grandma always seemed to see the good in every one, including Papa. She was patient and gentle with him even when he lost his temper, and could see a happy future no matter how dark things got at times. "All things work together for good to them that love God," she'd say just when it seemed there was nothing good anywhere. She knew her Bible by heart, and when she quoted from it we knew every word she said was true. I was so glad we could see her before we set out on that awful long trip to Iowa.

Grandpa's goodness was different. He made us mind our manners, as Mama did, and sometimes spoke sharply to us if we hadn't listened to something he told us to do. But we loved him just as much. Tonight I think all of us were proud of him for having the courage to "talk back" to Papa, and to do it without losing his temper and shouting the way Papa did. Papa was so mad when he left I thought suddenly that he might just get on the train and go on to Iowa without any of us. Now I wasn't sure I wanted him to do that. What good would it do? He'd sold the farm. Unless we could stay with Grandpa and Grandma for always.

We had finished dessert—my favorite peach-cobbler—when Papa came back. The way he marched in I knew he had done something he thought we wouldn't like.

"I've made arrangements with the freight office to ship my team and wagon tomorrow morning. I'll go on with them. Molly, you and the girls can stay here a week, but no longer. I'll need all of you to help finish the house and get ready for spring plowing." He acted like he'd forgotten Grandpa's scolding!

Grandma said, "Thank you, Sam. I'd been wishing Molly and the girls could stay a while. It may be a long time before I see them again. Iowa is quite a ways to go at my age." She got up from the table and started toward the kitchen. "Sam, would you help me with the pump? It doesn't seem to be working just right. Takes forever to get any water."

We all knew what she was up to. I'm sure Papa knew, too. But he said, "Sure", and followed her into the kitchen. Later, when Mama started clearing the table and pushed open the kitchen door, we could see Papa sitting at the table with a big plate of roast and potatoes and gravy before him. But he had his coat on!

It was always a mystery to me how fast Papa's "storms" could blow over. Tonight was no different. As soon as the dishes were done and put away, all of us sat in the parlor and listened to Papa talk about Iowa. Was this Grandpa's way of "smoothing the waters", I wondered? I had an idea Grandma wasn't very happy about all the Iowa talk, either, but she listened without saying anything against the place. And when she talked with us girls before she sent us up to bed, she made us feel we were going on a grand adventure. "God will be with you, all the way. Remember that."

I went to bed sure that everything *was* going to be all right. With Grandma and Grandpa and Mama, and God, too, I guessed all of us could put up with a papa like Papa.

CHAPTER III
1890

How Grandma and Grandpa could be so calm and cheerful about putting us on the train and sending us off to Iowa I couldn't understand. Didn't they *know* they might never see us again? Tears came into my eyes just thinking how awful it would be never to see *them* again. But Grandma went right on talking about the grand adventure we were going to have. Even Elsie became more cheerful, and carried the new straw suitcase Grandpa had bought for us without being told to do it. Vina carried the lunch and I the carpet-bag. Mama had her hands full with Lucy.

We marched down the platform, Mama leading the way. Her head was high but I knew she was worried. I'd heard her talking with Grandma last night.

"We shall have to change trains twice," she said. "Once at Streator and again in Chicago. I'm not worried about the change at Streator as much as the change in Chicago. We have to change stations there as well as trains. That will mean going by horse-car or cab from Dearborn Station to North Western's station at Eighth and Wells Streets."

"Best you take a cab, Molly, even if it does cost a little more," Grandma advised.

I thought the horse-car would be more exciting. But I'd never ridden in a cab *or* horse-car, so either would be a new adventure.

As the train roared in I forgot about both. There were last minute hugs and advice, and pretty soon we were settled onto green plush seats looking out the window at Grandma and Grandpa waving goodbye. The train chug-chugged slowly out of the station, then clickety-clacked over the rails as it went faster and faster.

"Gee, we must be going awful fast," Vina exclaimed.

"We sure are, young lady," the conductor said as he punched our tickets. "This train averages thirty-five miles an hour."

"And it goes up and down and sideways too," Vina giggled.

The conductor grinned at her. "That's the part of the ride you don't have to pay for." He handed the punched tickets to Mama, and moved on down the aisle.

Mama glanced at the window covered with thick February

frost. "I'm almost glad I can't see out. I don't think I'd like to see things fly by that fast." I knew she was thinking what I was. That each mile was taking us farther and farther away from Grandma and Grandpa, into a wild new country. To keep from thinking about that I looked around the elegant coach.

None of us girls had ever been on a railroad coach before. The green plush seats and brass lamps swinging from the ceiling as if they might fall any minute, made it an exciting place. We swayed with the train's movements and bounced a little when it went over a bump. It *was* kinda like a road, I thought. Even those silvery rails had bumps in them. Mama wiped the soot off the brown window sill with a piece of newspaper. It did no good. As soon as the brakeman opened the stove door to put on more coal a cloud of black smoke rose to the ceiling then settled soot on everything. When the train rounded a curve cinders rained against the rattling windows.

The water can on a little shelf near the stove fascinated me. It had a spigot and a chain with a tin cup attached. I watched the passengers smack their lips and the men lick their mustaches after each visit to the water can.

"May I have a drink, Mama?"

"There's a jar of buttermilk and a tin cup in the lunch basket."

"Couldn't I just have some water out of the spigot?"

Mama looked at the unshaven man with tobacco-stained mustache swaying back to his seat from the water can, and shook her head. "You'd better wait until we get to Streator, or have buttermilk," she said firmly.

Vina was making pictures on the frosted window. Elsie whispered to me. "See that handsome man with the derby hat in the third seat ahead? I'll bet he's a drummer. Do you know what a drummer is?"

I nodded. Elsie didn't believe me. "Bet you don't. He's *not* someone who plays a drum. He travels and sells things. You didn't know that, did you?"

"I did so. I heard Papa and Uncle Phil talking about them once."

Mama broke up the argument. "We'll be in Streator pretty

soon, girls. Put on your coats and wrap up well. We change trains there."

The station at Streator was heated by a big pot-bellied stove. We stood close to it waiting for our train. The station man said it would be along any minute. Mama told us to stay by the stove and she'd watch for the train near the door. Pretty soon we heard her exclaim, "Why, Phil! Where did you come from?"

Sure enough. It was Uncle Phil. But we wouldn't have recognized him if Mama hadn't. He was all dressed up in a black suit with a silk neck scarf, and wore a buffalo-hide overcoat.

"Molly! What a nice surprise." He didn't sound really surprised, though. "I'm on my way to Chicago."

"Well, you're an answer to prayer for sure. We have to change trains here and I've been dreading it."

"Dread no more, Madame," he said and made a little bow to Mama. "I'm going your way, too. I'll be able to help you and the girls across Chicago and onto the right train at Wells Street."

Elsie spoke up. "How did you know we were going to be on this train, and about Wells Street Station?"

Just then the train whistled. If Uncle Phil answered we couldn't hear him. He carried the straw suitcase and carpetbag. Mama carried Lucy and helped us onto the train. It was a much fancier one. Mama and Uncle Phil and Lucy sat together. Elsie and Vina and I took the seat ahead of them.

"I just can't get over your coming along when you did, Phil," Mama said. "But I'm certainly glad you did. I've never ridden on a horse-car, but the children were so excited about it I decided to take it instead of a cab."

"The horse-car is all right in good weather, Molly, but not very pleasant in this kind of weather. We'd best take the cab to Wells Street."

"Well, if you think so, Phil . . . ."

Elsie snickered. "Can you kids keep a secret?" she whispered. We told her we could and huddled close. "All right, then. Prove it by not telling Papa we ran into Uncle Phil. And stop looking over the back of the seat! Mama can take care of herself."

When we got to Chicago Uncle Phil found a cab for us

and helped us into it. It was crowded but we didn't mind. We pressed our faces against the small window but we couldn't see very much. It was raining. Mama and Uncle Phil talked in low tones. He stayed with us at the Wells Street station until our train came. Just before it roared in, he dug into his big overcoat pocket and brought out four small pink-and-green striped bags of rock candy. By the time we had finished examining them, Uncle Phil was gone and Mama was wiping her eyes.

"Wasn't it wonderful Uncle Phil happened to be going to Chicago today?" Vina remarked, popping a piece of rock candy into her mouth.

"Happened, my eye!" Elsie mumbled.

But Mama must have heard her. "That will be enough from you, young lady!"

It was a restless night for all of us except Lucy. Mama made a bed for her on one of the seats and covered her with her coat. I must have slept in spite of the train's bouncing over so many miles. I was awakened by the conductor calling loudly, "Stebbinsville!" I rubbed my eyes and shivered.

Light dimly penetrated the frosty coach windows. The stove glowed and spread a kind of smoky warmth. Why couldn't we just stay on and go back to Grandma's? Outside there would be only a land without trees, blizzards all winter long, and in summer prairie grass as high as Lucy's head. And holes in the ground instead of houses.

Mama told me to button my coat tightly about my throat and buckle my overshoes. Vina and Elsie already were bundled up and eager to get off. Other passengers were pushing toward the door each trying to get ahead of the other. Pretty soon I was standing on the station platform beside Mama and the others. The sharp cold wind against my face slapped me awake.

"At least there's a wooden depot," Elsie mumbled. "Can't we go inside, Mama, out of the cold?"

"Papa should be here with the wagon any minute. Best we wait here a while."

I jumped up and down to keep my feet warm and looked down the platform. There was no sign of Papa and the team and wagon. Around the corner of the depot I could see a few unpainted buildings. They looked as gray as the overcast

40

sky. I felt a little better, though, when I spied a few small trees. Their branches were bare of course, and they did look more like bony fingers reaching up from the snowy ground than little trees. I thought about the awful dream I had had the night Papa returned from Iowa and told us about the sod houses. But maybe he was only fooling us. He had said there were no trees, and there were!

We were still shivering on the windy platform when a big jolly-looking bearded man came toward us. "You must be Mrs. Bullard," he said, very friendly-like. "I'm Ethan Stone, Ma'am. Sam couldn't come in to meet you. He and the neighbors are fixing up a place for you to live, so he sent me to fetch you. I live just up the road a piece from your place."

Mama hesitated. How could Papa do such an awful thing? Sending a stranger to meet us! But Mama must have decided it was all right. She said politely, "That's very kind of you, Mr. Stone."

"No trouble, Mrs. Bullard. Sam said to bring you straight home. He's mighty anxious to see you. But you must be tired after that long trip. A few hours of rest at the Stebbins House will do you all good. That's our hotel, Ma'am."

"Well . . . I'm not sure . . ." Mama looked worried.

Mr. Stone laughed. "It's all right, lady. You'll find me quite a proper man, with a wife of my own. Besides, I've got some business to tend to that'll take me most of the morning. By noon you'll be rested and it'll be warmer for the trip."

"Very well, Mr. Stone. We must wait somewhere until you're ready and it's certainly too cold to wait in the station."

I remembered then what Papa had told us about the hotel. Mama must have forgotten! "Is that the hotel with no stairs, Mr. Stone?" I asked.

"What's she talking about, Ma'am? Of course the hotel has stairs."

Mama smiled. "I'm sure it does. Come along, children!"

The Stebbins House was only a little way from the station. Mr. Stone made arrangements with the manager for a large room with two beds. Mama bolted the door and checked the windows. While we took off our coats and overshoes she poured water from a big blue-flowered pitcher into the wash basin and washed Lucy's face and her own. Then it was our

41

turn. Mama and Lucy lay down on one bed and both were asleep in no time in spite of our whispered chatter. After a while we stretched out on the other bed. Everyone slept but me. I was too excited, and a little bit worried. I kept thinking about what Elsie had told Vina and me about hotels. How she knew I couldn't imagine. None of us had ever been in one. She said hotels were wicked places with gamblers and drummers and show girls with painted faces. They danced and drank with the men, and sometimes the men fought and shot each other. And there was always loud music and a lot of noise and swearing. I listened now for the loud music and gun shots. All I could hear was Mama's snoring. Elsie *had* been teasing us with those stories! I got up and tiptoed to the window. All I could see was an endless blanket of snow and a few small houses nearby, all huddled together like they were trying to keep each other warm.

We had finished our sandwiches and milk when Mr. Stone knocked on the door. He was ready when we were, he said. Mama let him take the carpet-bag and suitcase while she made sure each of us was bundled well against the cold.

Mr. Stone's bobsled was new and shiny with red runners and a box three boards high. The bottom was covered with clean fresh straw, and there was a heavy horseblanket to wrap up in. When he came out of the hotel he brought two heated stones, well wrapped, and put them at our feet. Mama tucked the blanket around us.

The skies had cleared. The noonday sun gave enough warmth to soften the bite of the wind. I watched the little town fade into the distance. The buildings got smaller and smaller until I could see only smoke from the chimneys. All around us the snow sparkled in the sunlight like a big blanket of stars. If there were any fences the snow must be deep enough to cover them. I didn't see one. The bobsled made its own road. The horses trotted sure-footed over the crusty snow.

Once the road dipped into a slight hollow and we passed a little grove of trees. Their ice-covered branches shivered in the wind. So . . . there were trees in Iowa after all! I hoped the little grove was close to our new farm. But I guess it wasn't. The sun was going down when Mr. Stone stopped the horses and we scrambled to the side of the sled to see our new home.

CHAPTER IV
1890

When Papa returned from his first trip to the new country he had spent the whole evening talking about the fine, comfortable houses the Iowan Land Company was building for new settlers.

Mama listened for a long time without saying anything. Then she said quietly, "We *have* a fine, comfortable house right here, Sam. Why must we go hundreds of miles looking for another?"

This made Papa mad. "It's progress, Molly. Can't you understand that? There's a whole new world out there and we have a chance to be a part of it. Pioneers, helping America grow."

"Seems to me we've done enough pioneering for a while, Sam, building this farm and this house. The children are getting big enough for other things besides weeding and hoeing. Are you forgetting there's another . . . . ."

"Of course I haven't. The new house will be ready long before that. And you'll agree I was right about selling this farm when you see that big new country. Lots of space and the best soil . . . . ."

So the farm was sold. Now we were here in Papa's "big new country" peering over the side of a bobsled for a look at our wonderful new house. And there was nothing! Nothing but snow-covered fields and something that looked like a big snowdrift.

"Why are we stopping here?" Mama asked.

Mr. Stone looked surprised. "Didn't Sam write you the new house isn't finished? We've fixed up this old soddy for you until it's ready. You'll be right cozy in it, Mrs. Bullard. Lived in one myself while I was building my own house."

So we *were* going to live like prairie dogs afterall!

"How long will it take to finish the house?" Mama asked slowly.

"Oh, I'd say you should be able to get into it in a coupla weeks. It won't be finished by then but you'll be able to live in it." Mr. Stone tied the reins and jumped down.

Mama made no move to get out. We waited to see what she was going to do. Finally she gave a big sigh and handed Lucy down to Mr. Stone. We scrambled out of our warm straw nest but we didn't have time to see much. Papa came running toward us and grabbed Mama and kissed her right in front of Mr. Stone.

"Gosh, I've missed you!" he kept saying over and over.

Mama's face got red. She pushed Papa away. "Oh, Sam, the baby! The girls . . . . ."

Papa hadn't seemed to notice us until then. Now he hugged and kissed all of us like he had missed us too. When I looked at Mama she was smiling. I guessed everything was going to be all right, but I still didn't want to live in a soddy.

Papa carried Lucy and held onto Mama's arm. We followed. He led us along a newly shoveled path toward the big snowdrift. It had a door. Mama and Papa and Lucy went through it. Elsie, Vina, and I just stood there in the freezing wind. We were cold but how could we get warm inside a snow bank? Then Papa opened the door again to see what had happened to us. Warmth flowed out and lamplight welcomed us.

Inside we saw only one room with clay plastered walls. A horseblanket hung on one of them. The only window was small like the one in our old barn, and was too high up to see out of. Drifted snow covered half the glass. Mama took our coats and hung them on pegs near the stove. She put Lucy on the bed and took off her shoes and stockings and rubbed her little feet. "They're like ice, child." Lucy laughed. Rubbing tickled her feet. Mama left her on the bed. It was the one from Mama's and Papa's room on the old farm. It had little brass balls on each bedpost that could be taken off to polish. Lucy began twisting at one of them the way she did at home.

"Stop that, Lucy!" Elsie snapped. "It makes me nervous."

"Leave her alone, Elsie," Mama said. "It's one thing at least to make her feel at home."

Elsie didn't talk back. She was probably wondering, as I was, how anything could be right in a cave with nothing but snow for a hundred miles. Papa was prancing around more like a colt, I thought, than a stallion. He grabbed Mama again

44

and kissed her. This time Mama didn't push him away. She smiled! "You'd better ask Mr. Stone in, Sam. I'll make some hot coffee."

Papa let go of her and started for the door. "By Jasper, I forgot all about him!"

Mr. Stone and the bobsled were gone. Papa shrugged when he came back inside and told us about it, "I guess he thought he'd be in the way. He knew how much I've missed you."

"But you didn't even thank him! Nor did I. You must have missed me," Mama scolded. But she didn't look or sound angry.

Papa grinned. "A man's not supposed to cook for himself and sleep alone." He started toward her.

Mama moved to the other side of the table and picked up the kerosene lamp. The chimney was blackened. She set about cleaning it. "I'll need more firewood, Sam, before I start supper." Papa didn't have to be asked twice. He took a galvanized bucket from behind the stove and went outside. When he came back he had a bucket of coal. "I guess I forgot to tell you we don't have firewood here. We use coal. It has to be hauled out from town."

Mama didn't complain. She was still smiling as she fixed supper.

We were awakened the next morning by the rattle of the range grate. Papa, not Mama, was shaking down the ashes before setting the new fire. Mama was still snugly under the covers.

"You kids stay in bed 'til the room warms up a little," he said.

Iowa was beginning to seem more like heaven every minute!

Mama waited a while then got up and made coffee and set the teakettle on. She let us stay in bed until the smell of coffee filled the ugly room and a kettle of oatmeal simmered on the back of the stove. We dressed behind the stove, hopping from one foot to the other because the floor was still cold.

"Hurry along, girls. Papa'll be back in a minute for breakfast."

"Where'd he go?" Elsie asked. "Where could anyone go in this snow-wilderness? Not even a house to live in!"

Mama spoke firmly. "I want all of you to listen to me. I

know you're disappointed about the house not being ready. So am I. But Papa says it will be in a couple of weeks and it isn't going to kill us to live here that long. I wish we could have stayed in Saunemin, but we didn't. We're here, and it'll be a lot easier for all of us if we try to make the best of it."

Papa came in before we could say anything. He brought another bucket of coal and dumped an armful of sticks into the woodbox. "Not much kindling about 'til the snow clears a little, but I dug out what I could. It'll be dry by morning."

We ate breakfast in silence. That is, we were silent. Mama got in a word now and then. Papa was off on his favorite subject—this fine, new land! I glanced at Elsie. She rolled her eyes upward and sighed. Vina saw her and giggled. Papa didn't pay any attention to us. He was talking about big crops and big money. He hadn't changed at all!

Breakfast over, I asked, "May we go outside and look around, Mama?"

Papa answered for her. "Go ahead, but don't stay too long. I forgot to tell you, Molly, some of the neighbors are coming over today to help clean out the back room." He got up and pulled aside the horseblanket.

Behind it was a narrow opening into what once must have been another room. Now it was just a dark hole filled with dirt and junk. Some of the roof had caved in. It would be a back-breaking job to clean all that out. Besides, what was the use? We'd be in the new house before we could make that room decent enough to sleep in. No one said anything, not even Mama.

Elsie and Vina and I put on our coats and stocking-caps and overshoes and went outside. It was awfully cold. For a while the sun on sparkling fields of snow blinded us. When we could see more clearly we saw the frame of our new house sticking up from the snow about fifty feet from the soddy. Papa's boots had made a path. We followed it. The crusty snow squeaked and crunched under our overshoes. Once Vina slipped and sat down hard. Her laughter echoed across the fields.

Elsie stared at the unfinished house in disgust. "Two weeks, my eye! We'll be living in that dirty soddy until spring. And who knows *when* spring gets to this part of the country?"

I couldn't believe that. "Maybe not, Elsie," I said to cheer myself. "Even Mr. Stone said it would be ready in two weeks and he ought to know."

"He'd have to say that, wouldn't he? If Papa told him to."

Looking at the skeleton house with snow drifted halfway up the side timbers, I thought Elsie was probably right. Maybe Mr. Stone was only trying to make us feel better about the soddy when he said that. He seemed like a kind man. Still, even with neighbors helping Papa I couldn't see how the house could be finished in two weeks. It didn't even have walls yet, let alone a roof. We'd have to live in that awful soddy for a long time!

Vina hadn't said a word. I don't think she'd even looked at the house. She was having too much fun sliding on the hard-packed snow and throwing snowballs at us. Elsie and I didn't feel like playing. Slowly we started back to the soddy, the only home we had.

In the full light of day we saw that the soddy *was* just a dugout in the side of a sloping mound, now buried in snow except for the front path Papa had shoveled. Walking back, Elsie told me how a soddy was made. Pieces of grassy sod from the fields were used as building blocks to make walls high enough for people the size of Papa. Then the whole thing was covered with old boards and cornstalks and dead branches if there were any, and finally a thick layer of earth, wetted down, so the summer sun would bake it almost as hard as bricks.

"And in winter, with the snow on top of all that, it's as snug as a house."

"How do you know all that?" I never could be sure that Elsie wasn't making up stories just to sound important.

"Oh, I know a lot of things you don't. When you get older you'll know them too."

Smoke curled from a piece of stove-pipe sticking up from the mound of snow. "A soddy is sure a funny-looking place to live in," I said.

We had been back only a few minutes when there was a knock on the door. Papa called, "Come in!" It was Mr. Stone. With him was a plump, pretty woman with pink cheeks and taffy-colored hair. "My wife, Hilda," he said, beaming proudly.

47

She greeted Mama with a big smile and talked in a funny way.

"I bring for dinner," she said, and set a big copper kettle on the stove. She took the cover off a bowl of white stuff and set it on the table. It looked like cottage cheese, but she called it something else. *"Hosenpfeffer* and *schmeercase.* You work too hard, maybe stork mistake make."

She unwound a red fascinator from about her head and throat. Thick yellow braids circled her head. Her eyes were blue like cornflowers and they seemed to be laughing even when she wasn't. Papa jumped up and took her coat and hung it up. Mama introduced each of us. Mrs. Stone shook hands with us like we were grownups. Papa and Mr. Stone went outside.

"Fine family you haf', Mrs. Bullard. Pretty too, like their mama." And she laughed like it made her happy just to look at us. "Where our men go?" she asked.

"To clear the snow from where the roof of the other room used to be," Mama explained.

"Goot! We start inside maybe?"

She and Mama moved furniture to make a path to the door behind the horseblanket. Vina kept Lucy out of the way. Elsie and I washed the dishes and made the beds, giggling to ourselves over the funny way Mrs. Stone talked.

"Why does she talk that way?" I whispered.

"Because she came from Germany."

"How do you know?"

Elsie tossed her head and didn't answer. We could hear the sharp sound of a pick axe hacking away over our heads, and hear Papa and Mr. Stone talking. Papa's voice sounded like it came from the back room. Mama said, "I guess they got down through the roof. They're digging in that awful mess."

It was almost noon when Papa and Mr. Stone came through the opening behind the blanket. Mama and Mrs. Stone dished up the food. We squatted about the table picnic-fashion, and ate quickly. There was a lot of work to be done.

"We'd better get the roof fixed first, Ethan," Papa said.

"Good idea. I'll bring some timbers from the new house. How many do you think we'll need?"

"Oh, three or four ought to be enough. The girls can bring the boards when we get the beams in place."

Mr. Stone went out but he didn't take a shovel. He was going to need one to find any lumber in all that snow. I guess he found one at the new house because he was back in a few minutes with three timber-beams. Now it was our turn.

"You kids go back with him," Papa ordered. "You can drag some of the boards if you can't carry them. We have to get this roof on before dark."

Mr. Stone dug the boards out of the snow but we girls did all the carrying. After the first trip he had to help Papa with the roof. As soon as it was in place Papa put Elsie and me to work carrying a basketful of dirt at a time from the back room. Mr. Stone handed it up to Papa to spread in layers over the boards.

It was beginning to get dark when they finished. All of us hovered around the stove rubbing our numbed fingers. Mama had coffee for the men and hot chocolate for us. When I sat down at the table I felt like my bones were frozen and my skin cracking. My back ached. Elsie groaned every time she moved.

Papa said, "Ethan and I have done the hard work. You women and kids can clean up the rest. I'm going over to Ethan's place and help him with his chores."

He hadn't changed! But he soon found out he couldn't order Hilda Stone around the way he did us.

She said firmly, "*Nein!* Ethan help here. I shovel. You un' Ethan carry. Molly boss." She turned to us. "*Kinder* keep coffee hot."

But a glance at Papa must have warned Mrs. Stone Papa would never let Mama boss him, so she did that herself, and to everyone's surprise, Papa didn't argue.

"Light lantern. Bring basket. Dirt carry." Both men obliged without complaining. Mama held the lantern and kept Lucy from underfoot. We watched and kept the fire going. With the door open so much of the time, and the cold coming in from that dark back room, we needed all the heat the range could give.

Hilda Stone seemed never to tire. She laughed most of the time as she bent above the shovel. She seemed to enjoy digging. Maybe having two strong men to carry out the dirt had something to do with it. "Is *goot!*" she said as each basket was filled.

49

"See! Hilda Stone on one end shovel, America on other!" And then she'd laugh until the sound echoed in that awful dark room.

Again she plunged the shovel into the hard earth. This time there was a dull, hollow sound. "Move closer the lantern, Molly!" She scraped ·the dirt away with her shovel and suddenly laughed again. "A bone! Dog dig here too I bet!" She went on scraping away the dirt. Mr. Stone took the lantern and squatted down to throw more light on the place. We girls crowded close in the doorway. Maybe it was buried treasure! If it was maybe Papa would take all of us back to Virginia where they used to live.

"*Gott im Himmel!*" Mrs. Stone cried. "People bones!"

Mama quickly pulled us away from the door. But not before I'd caught a glimpse of a white skull.

"Pioneers probably," Papa said calmly. "Indians musta got 'em."

Mrs. Stone came out of the cavern mumbling strange words to herself. Mr. Stone followed, carrying the lantern. Papa took it from him and went back inside. When he came out a few minutes later he said, "Yep! They're human bones all right. Hard to tell much else, though."

The Stones said nothing. Mama started to cry. "Sam, please take us back to Illinois! Please!"

"Stop that, Molly! I'm *not* taking you back. A Bullard *never* turns back!"

Mama stopped crying. "Then *you* can go on alone, Sam Bullard! I won't bring up my family in this . . . this *boneyard!*"

Papa put down the lantern and took Mama by the shoulders. "Come to your senses, Molly! Sure you've had a shock. But where's your spunk, your pioneer spirit? Lots of women fought real Indians to settle this country, and you're scared of a few bones."

"Some of those women *lost* the fight, too. And their brave men left them where they fell. Not even a decent grave!"

Papa quieted down. "That was a long time ago. There are no Indians here now."

"No, but a lot of other things just as bad." Mama's voice rose in anger. "Sickness and childbirth without a doctor. Freezing weather with no wood to burn. And no place to live but in these . . . these *tombs!*" We'd never seen Mama so upset, and we'd never heard her talk this way to Papa. "There that woman lies, a sacrifice to some man's ego. And where's her man? Probably with another wife in some comfortable home back East bragging about how *he* opened the West!"

"Stop it, Molly! You're getting hysterical over a few bones. We don't even know they're a woman's bones. But if they are, *she* wasn't a whimpering female. She stuck with her man."

"Well, *this* 'whimpering female' is taking her children back to civilization before they end up bones in a soddy!"

"You're doing no such thing. Now come on, let's get that back room cleaned out." He went back into the dark hole.

Mrs. Stone whispered something to her husband and he went outside. She came over and put her arm around Mama's shoulder. "You un' *kinder* come home mit me tonight, Molly. Ethan stay here with Sam."

She brought Lucy's coat and hood and put them on her. Mama got her coat and we put on ours on the way to the door. We *had* to get out of here before Papa could stop us! How could he even want us to live in this awful place?

By the time Papa came charging out after us we were all in the bobsled with Mrs. Stone. "Molly Bullard, you come back here! A man has some rights . . !" But Mama was in the bottom of the sled out of sight, holding Lucy.

Mrs. Stone slapped the lines and threw back her head and yelled something in that funny language. Papa ran after the sled and tried to grab the endgate. She slapped the lines again, harder. The team leaped forward. Papa missed the endgate and sprawled on his face in the snow. When we looked back Papa was brushing the snow from his eyes. Mr. Stone was laughing and he waved until we were out of sight.

Spending the night at the Stone's house gave us a better idea of the kind of place ours would be if it ever got finished. Mama was her old self the next morning. "I'm sorry, Hilda," I heard her say. "I just couldn't take any more. And I'm *not* going back to that soddy."

"We see, Molly. Come now, breakfast eat. Then we talk."

Listening to her as we ate breakfast, I guess Mama was convinced things *would* be a lot different when our house was built. Mrs. Stone said the house would be just like hers, and *it* was comfortable enough, even pretty. All houses built by the Iowan Land Company, it seemed, were exactly alike. Each was a frame building divided almost in the middle by a stairway, with two bedrooms upstairs, one larger than the other. Downstairs there were three rooms—a kitchen with buttery, sitting-room, and bedroom. But Mrs. Stone had changed things to suit herself. Her sitting-room had been turned into a dining-room, and what was supposed to be the bedroom was her sitting-room.

Mama asked, "Why do they build them all alike? Why can't they be built to suit the people who are going to live in them?"

"Save money, maybe. But, is *goot* I t'ink. Every house is home, *nicht wahr?*"

Mama wasn't sure about that. She said she wanted a dining-room, of course, but with the size of her family we needed three bedrooms. "Maybe we could divide the larger bedroom upstairs into two rooms. Then if we ate in the kitchen I could have a sitting-room *and* a parlor. What do you think, Hilda?"

Mrs. Stone shrugged. "Parlor? *Vas ist?*" Mama explained. "Vat use ist parlor ven you haf' sitting-room?"

"To you, Hilda, maybe no use. You don't have growing daughters. Girls need a nice place to entertain gentlemen friends when they come calling."

Hilda laughed and winked at Elsie. "Haystack maybe cheaper way!" She told how Ethan Stone had courted her while they worked in the fields of her father's farm in Wisconsin. "Now ve haf' fine farm. Much room to live and haf' babies. Why *freulein* need parlor, Molly Bullard?" She tossed her head and laughed.

Mama's face got red. "Elsie, you and Ann go upstairs and make the beds. It will be lunch time before we know it."

We obeyed, but I left the stairway door open a crack, and we were in no hurry to make beds. We sat on the steps and listened. We could see Vina and Lucy playing with dominoes at the dining-room table. Mama and Mrs. Stone were in the sitting-room, out of our sight, but we could hear plainly enough.

"How you trap Sam, Molly?"

52

We scooted down a step to hear better.

"I don't think I 'trapped' Sam, Hilda. I just made sure he courted me properly."

"How you do that?"

"Well, the first time I saw Sam Bullard he was riding down Main street on a beautiful black horse. I didn't know who he was but I thought he was the most dashing man I'd ever seen in his wide-brimmed hat and fancy boots with spurs. And the way he sat his horse was something to see! Tall in the saddle like he was *somebody,* and I knew he must be. That night at dinner my father told Mother that Sam Bullard was back, and explained that he was one of the young men who had gone north after the war to try to get back some of what they had lost. The man I'd seen riding down Main street *had* to be Sam Bullard. And I *had* to meet him. But I couldn't let my parents know I was attracted to him. That wouldn't have been lady-like, and Mother was very strict about good manners. So I had to wait for a proper introduction. But just in case I *might* run into him walking down the street I made sure I looked my best each time I went out." Mama laughed. "So you see, Hilda, I didn't exactly set a trap for him; I just waited to be invited to the right party!"

Mrs. Stone laughed heartily. "I t'ink maybe haystack an' party *not* different!"

"Oh, but they are, Hilda. In Virginia everything had to be very proper."

Mrs. Stone didn't say anything for a while, then, "*Nein*, Molly Bullard. Hilda not like Virginia way. Too slow!"

"That depends upon what you like most," Mama said. "The Minuet or the Virginia Reel."

"Vas ist?"

"Well, in a Minuet the gentleman leads and the lady follows. But in the Virginia Reel it's a kind of free-for-all. You just dance as fast as the fiddler can fiddle."

Hilda Stone's laughter echoed through the whole house. "*Joost* like haystack, *ja!*"

It was exciting to know someone like Mrs. Stone. She talked funny and her ways of doing things were often quite different from those Mama had taught us. But she was very good for Mama. She was strong and knew how to live in this

53

rough new land and be happy. Mama was strong too, but she was gentle. Some things, I thought, needed more than a strong back to be endured. Like when Papa had made me drown all of Tabby's kittens, and I had cried for days. But I knew Mama would not go back to Illinois as she had threatened to do last night. We would stay here and have to live in that awful place. Maybe this was Mama's kind of strength—to make the best of what she dreaded most.

With Mrs. Stone to talk to, Mama seemed more content. After lunch that day, we gathered around the big base-burner in Hilda Stone's pretty sitting-room. She and Mama talked about our new house but they hadn't said a word about where we were going to live in the meantime. Where else was there to live but that old soddy?

Then Mama was saying, "I'll put up with hardship, cold, even hunger, Hilda. But no power under God's heaven is going to make the children and me live in that soddy!"

No one said anything. We heard the kitchen door open.

Mrs. Stone whispered, "Maybe our men not like boneyards so pretty goot, either!"

Mr. Stone was alone when he came into the sitting-room. "Where is Sam?" Mama asked. I wondered what kind of mood Papa would be in when we had to face him again.

"He's in the kitchen. I think he's just a *little* bit afraid of you, Molly."

"Is *goot!*" Hilda Stone said.

Ethan Stone smiled. "Maybe. Sometimes, anyway. But let's give Sam the credit he deserves. He's had time to think things over and agrees the soddy is not a fit place for women and girls. Once maybe, but not now. None of us had any idea what was in that back room until we started digging. So here's our plan. In a couple of weeks you can get into your new house. Until then, we'll bring one of your beds from the soddy and put it in the sitting-room for you and Sam. The girls can use that small bedroom upstairs. If we move things around a little there will be room for a cot. Is that all right with you, Hilda?"

"*Ja. Ja. Goot!* You like, Molly?"

"It would be wonderful, Hilda, but won't it crowd you too much?"

54

"*Nein.* You come! Ve fix up fine." She whispered something to Mr. Stone and he called to Papa. "Molly says you're welcome if your nose is clean! That's her way of telling you she's not mad at you any more."

Papa stood a minute in the doorway, then came on into the sitting-room. Hilda put out her hand, "Ve be *goot* neighbors, Sam Bullard. Molly fine woman." She turned and winked at Mama. "*Ja,* he still strong un' handsome. A boy like he you be haf'in'!"

The way Papa looked at Hilda Stone I knew he wasn't mad at her any more, either. And, glory be! We *weren't* going to have to live in the soddy!

Living with Uncle Ethan and Aunt Hilda, as we now called them, was fun. Aunt Hilda was always happy. Nothing ever seemed a calamity to her. She'd just laugh, and pretty soon everyone else was laughing with her. Mama seemed embarrassed sometimes by things Aunt Hilda said in front of us girls, so we didn't let on we knew what she meant. Still, we learned things about life Mama might not have told us. Not then, anyway.

Papa never would have admitted it, but by now it was pretty clear to all of us that he couldn't have "pioneered" without Ethan Stone's help and advice. He had plenty to do on his own farm, but almost every day he came over to help Papa. The snow was still deep around the new house and the wind was very cold. Building was slow, and when it snowed—which it seemed to do most of the time—they couldn't work on the house at all. Some days when the weather wasn't too bad, Papa and Uncle Ethan would drive into town and bring back more coal, fence-posts, wire and seed-grain. Papa said as soon as the crops were in and the house was so we could live in it he intended to fence the farm.

"Can't that wait a while, Sam?" Mama asked. "Most farms here don't have them. They don't seem to need fencing. Maybe they will in time, but now it seems like a waste of time and money."

"Got to do it sooner or later. Just as well get it done. Besides, I like to know where my boundaries are."

Mama didn't say any more to him about it. But to Aunt

Hilda she said, "He's a proud man, Hilda. I think a fence is just something to remind him how much of this land he owns."

The weather stayed cold. It snowed almost every day, some days all day and night or for several days without stopping. It was going to be a lot longer than two weeks before we got the house finished. I hoped Aunt Hilda didn't mind. It looked like it would be spring before we had a place of our own. February went out "like a lion". Forty-mile winds sent walls of snow across the prairies. Sometimes we couldn't even see the barn from Aunt Hilda's kitchen window.

So we weren't prepared for the "miracle". Suddenly the snow stopped, the winds died down and were warm as spring. The snow began to disappear like magic.

"It's the Chinook wind," Uncle Ethan explained. "It comes about this time every spring. A few days of this and the land will be ready for the plow."

But not even Uncle Ethan expected what the Chinook wind brought that spring.

With most of the snow gone in a few days, Papa and Uncle Ethan and two other neighbors worked on our house. The ground was still too wet for plowing. Elsie and Vina and I carried boards, nails and tools. Hilda handed them up to the men on the roof. Mama and Lucy watched from the doorway of the storage shed the land company had built last fall. It was sturdy and gave shelter from the wind.

Papa called to Vina. "Go get that little saw I left in the soddy."

Vina hesitated. The soddy was full of darkness and bones. Mama must have thought of that too. "Sam, don't send that child down there. I'll get the saw."

"*Nein!*" Aunt Hilda said. "Molly sit. Sam vill get saw."

For a minute Papa looked like he was going to yell at her but he didn't. Pretty soon he climbed down, grumbling, "Molly, you've lived with Hilda too long! Next week we move!" He started toward the soddy. Vina saw him coming and got out of the way.

We watched until he reached the door of the soddy, then saw him jump back.

"Ethan, Hilda, Molly! Come quick!"

Uncle Ethan came down the ladder two rungs at a time.

When we reached the soddy Papa was standing by the door in water up to his ankles.

"Help get this furniture out," he yelled.

Water from the melting snow had dripped through the temporary roof, flooding the place. Tables, chairs and the other two beds stood in six inches of dirty water. Mama's rocker-cushions were soaked. So was the horseblanket over the back door opening. The worst damage was to the sacks of seed-grain Papa had stored in the front room of the soddy instead of the storage shed which he said he needed now for tools and lumber.

He waded in and got a shovel and dug a little ditch from the front door to let the water run out. Then, piece by piece, we carried the furniture up to the new house and piled it in the rooms that had a roof over them. Papa and Uncle Ethan put the sacks of seed-grain into Ethan's wagon. "We'll store them in my shed, Sam. It gets pretty warm in there. They should be dry enough in a few days for planting. I don't think you'll lose very much of it."

"Much obliged, Ethan. I sure hope you're right."

Papa marched back to the soddy. He looked mad enough to tear the place down. All he did was board up the door. It looked like we wouldn't have to live in that place ever again. But later, when the sun was hot and dry winds blew, Papa opened up the soddy and let it dry out, and used it again for storage.

Before the summer was over we had plenty of reason to be grateful for that old soddy.

While warm weather lasted Papa, Uncle Ethan and our neighbors worked hard to get the house in shape to live in. Plastering and papering, Papa said, could be done later. He seemed in a big hurry to get Mama away from Aunt Hilda before she became more independent.

There hadn't been room in the soddy for all our things when they arrived from Saunemin, so Papa had stored some of the furniture and boxes of dishes and things we didn't need, in the shed. We now carried these into the new house as soon as all the roof was on. It began to look more like a home, on the inside at least. Outside there was still much to be done. The houses built by the Land Company had only a narrow stoop in front and back. Aunt Hilda had added a front porch. Mama wanted both a front and back porch and for once Papa agreed with her.

He did a lot of wooden-swearing while he was setting up the kitchen range and fixing the stove-pipe. Mama made a fire and put on a pot of coffee. Soon the kitchen was warm and cozy. Her rocker was by the window and Aunt Hilda ordered her to use it. "Set and baby hold. Ve make house nice."

Mama must have been pretty tired because she didn't argue. Elsie and I unpacked boxes and baskets. Aunt Hilda, with some instructions from Mama, put the dishes in the cupboard and cooking utensils in place. Mama always kept things neat. "A place for everything and everything in its place," was her motto and she made sure we learned it too. After a while Papa and Uncle Ethan came in with the dining-room table and set it down in the middle of the kitchen floor.

Mama said "Sam. I've decided to use the sitting-room as a dining-room, the way Hilda does. We can use the downstairs bedroom for a sitting-room and divide the upstairs into three rooms. That will give us enough sleeping space and privacy until we can build on a couple more rooms."

Papa snorted the way he did when he was mad but he had

to be polite with Aunt Hilda there. "We don't need a dining-room, Molly. This is pioneer country."

The dining table remained in the kitchen. There would be a sitting-room and a bedroom downstairs and two bedrooms upstairs, just the way Papa wanted it. But as soon as Papa went out Mama said to Aunt Hilda, "We can change things later when I'm up and around again." I didn't know what she meant exactly, but she was smiling the way she always did when she was making secret plans.

It was snowing and cold the next morning. The false spring hadn't lasted very long. We girls huddled about the stove turning the pages of a big wallpaper sample book Aunt Hilda had lent to Mama. We had picked out a pattern for each room. If Mama liked the patterns maybe Papa would let us have what we all wanted. But that would depend upon the mood he happened to be in the day Mama went to buy the wallpaper.

Mama was sitting by the window knitting. We watched her, waiting for the right moment to show her our selections. Every little while she would put down her knitting and look off across the treeless snow-covered fields. I thought the stocking she was knitting looked awfully small even for Lucy. When she picked up her knitting again Elsie tiptoed over to her and put the wallpaper book in her lap. She looked up. "What's this, child?"

"We've picked out the wallpaper we want Papa to buy. Will you ask him to, Mama?"

"First, let's see what you've chosen."

We squatted on the floor beside her, turning the pages. "Isn't *this* simply beautiful, Mama?" I said. It was white with yellow daffodils. We'd picked it for our bedroom. "And this," Elsie exclaimed. It looked like a garden of little red roses and we'd all agreed it was the *only* right paper for the sitting room.

"They're all beautiful, girls. We'll see what Papa says." She smiled but I thought she looked very tired and worried. "Now we'd better fix dinner. Papa will be cold and hungry when he gets back from town."

A week passed. Mama said no more about the wallpaper and we didn't either. Papa was too busy outside the house to care about the inside. Uncle Ethan finished putting on the lath but that was as far as he got. Papa needed him outside. "We can plaster and paper any time. I want to get this porch on before we have to start plowing." But when the porch was finished there were other outside jobs. A corral to be built, and the big galvanized watering tank for the stock to be set in place. When these were done Papa started building the scaffolding for the windmill tower so it would be ready when the well was dug. Digging a well and post-holes had to wait for the ground to thaw. And as soon as it was thawed, Papa put all of us to work getting the crops in. All except Mama. There Aunt Hilda put her foot down!

I guess it was a good thing she did. One morning in early April Mama didn't get up for breakfast. Elsie cooked the oatmeal, made biscuits and fried eggs. As soon as we finished eating Papa took Vina and Lucy and me over to Aunt Hilda's. Elsie stayed with Mama. Aunt Hilda didn't seem surprised Mama was sick. When Papa said, "Molly needs you," she just nodded and said, "Is *goot,*" and put on her coat and overshoes and fascinator and followed him out.

Uncle Ethan said, "I'll saddle a horse and get the doctor."

"No need for that," Papa said. "Molly'll be all right with Hilda."

But right after Papa and Aunt Hilda left Uncle Ethan put on his coat and fur cap and said he was going for the doctor anyway. I wanted to ask him how sick Mama was but I didn't. He was in a hurry now, I'd ask when he got back.

It was almost noon when Uncle Ethan returned but Papa wasn't with him. When I asked about Mama he said, "Oh, she'll be up and around in no time, child." He brought a bowl of *schmeercase,* some cold cornbread and half an apple pie and set them on the table. "You know where the plates and glasses are, Ann. I'll get the milk from the cellar." Afterwards Vina and I washed the dishes, but today we didn't make a game of it the way we did at home. We were worried about Mama.

It was beginning to get dark when Papa came for us. As soon as we stepped into our kitchen Aunt Hilda came from the bedroom with a bundle in her arms. "See, *kinder!* New baby sister you haf'." She turned back the blanket to let us see. It looked awfully small and wrinkled and its face was so *red!*

"Where did it come from?" Vina asked.

"By the doctor she come," Aunt Hilda told her.

60

Just then a strange man came out of Mama's bedroom. He must have heard what she said. "Yes, ma'am, little ladies. Right out of this black bag." He held it up so we could see, and winked at Aunt Hilda.

"Is Mama very sick?" I asked.

He patted my shoulder and said just what Uncle Ethan had said. "Your Mama will be up and around in no time."

Elsie fixed the crib and drew it close to the range. Aunt Hilda put the baby down, tucked her in, and turned to us. "Your mama rest must haf' now. You all help, *ja?*" She glanced at Papa. I told her we would, but Papa didn't say anything.

Vina sighed. "My goodness! What an awful time for Mama to get sick! Just when we've got a new baby sister to take care of!"

Papa laughed. "You'd better make it a boy next time, Doc, or I'll get another doctor."

Aunt Hilda gave him a scowling look. "About next time you talk already!"

"A man *needs* sons, Hilda Stone. What good are girls to a farmer?"

She tossed her head. "Pretty *goot* I t'ink! Where else you get wifes and mamas?"

The doctor laughed. "She's got you there, Mr. Bullard." He put on his coat and picked up his bag. "I'll look in on your wife in a day or two."

When he had gone Papa poured himself a cup of coffee and sat down at the table. "Bring me a piece of that custard pie, will you, Hilda, before you go." She brought it and a cup of coffee for herself. "Nothing but girls, girls, girls," Papa mumbled through a mouthful of pie. "I'll swear, Hilda, I don't know what's wrong with Molly."

Aunt Hilda jumped up and stood there, hands on her hips, glaring at him. "Better you ask vat wrong with Sam Bullard!" Then she turned her back on him and came over to the cradle and squatted beside it, rocking the baby and talking to it. *"Goot* baby! Nice baby! Hilda haf' soon pretty baby *joost* like you!"

She put on her coat and overshoes, and gave instructions to Elsie.

"I'll take you home," Papa said.

"Nein. I take myself, Sam Bullard." She lifted her chin. *"Vat goot frauliens,* humph!"

Aunt Hilda came over every day while Mama was in bed. As the doctor had promised, Mama was up and around in a week. She said there wasn't time to rest with so much to be done, and Papa agreed with her. The weather was warm enough now to dry the plaster. At least Papa had promised to do that much. The papering, he said, could wait a while. But he and Elsie were busy with plowing and seeding, so both the plastering and papering waited. My job was to turn the fanning mill that cleaned the grain for planting. Papa shoveled it into gunnysacks and carried it to the field and poured it into the seeder. Elsie drove the driller back and forth, making sure the rows overlapped just enough to cover the ground evenly with seeds. Then came the harrowing, lengthwise and across, covering the seeds with rich dark soil and making the ground smooth so it would be easy to harvest in the fall.

All of us worked from sun-up to dark. Mama cooked and did the washing and took care of the baby. She had named her Mae. It was a pretty name and suited her, I thought. Her eyes were blue and her hair like May sunshine. Even little Lucy now had her chores. She could fetch and carry small things that saved Mama steps. Papa made sure there were no idle hands on the Bullard farm. The only rest Mama got that spring was when she sat in her rocker to nurse the baby. Then she hummed to herself her favorite hymn as she looked off across the fields.

> The Great Physician now is near
> The sympathizing Jesus.
> He speaks the drooping heart to cheer
> Oh, hear the voice of Jesus!

Her voice sounded sad but when she looked down at baby Mae sleeping peacefully, she smiled.

Gradually we learned to accept life as it was here on the open prairie. The house at last was finished, inside and outside, even the papering done. We had been allowed to have most of our selections, but papa insisted upon a different color on their bedroom, something not so "fancy," he said, and Mama gave in to that. Papa was now talking about planting trees and building fences. He also wanted a bigger barn, and we had to have a storm-cellar, he said, before cyclone weather was upon us. No one argued about that!

The big excitement that spring was watching the well-diggers. There was always danger of a cave-in. If that happened the well became a grave for the digger, and a new well would have to be started. The deeper our well got the more we held our breath each day until the digger came up, wet and muddy. At last the dangerous work was finished. The tower was set up and soon the windmill wheel whirred and glistened in the sunlight. It made a pleasant sound.

In spite of the endless work Papa found for us to do, spring on the prairie was a wondrous time. Suddenly there was a smooth green carpet as far as our eyes could see. Flowers sprang up from the dark soil dotting the fields with yellow and red and purple. Some of the flowers were different from any we had seen before. We made a game of seeing who could find the most new kinds. One morning Lucy burst into the house with a handful of soft fuzzy purple-tinted blossoms. "See what I found, Mama. What are they?"

"Wild crocus, darling. But let's call them May flowers. That will be easier for you to remember." She put them in a glass of water and set them in the middle of the dining table. "They are lovely, dear. Where did you find them?"

"In the meadow back of the barn. There's lots of them. I only picked a few. Was it all right to pick them, Mama?"

"Yes, dear. God sends them every spring to tell us winter is over. I think He also wants us to know there will always be another spring if we have faith."

I knew she was speaking to all of us, and to herself.

Some days, when I'd finished my part of the work, I was allowed to roam the prairie looking for wild asparagus and horseradish. Both had grown by the creek on our old farm. Here there were no creeks; at least I hadn't seen any. Maybe there was one in that little patch of trees we'd passed on the way to the new farm that first day. But that was too far to walk. Mama had promised to take us to town when the weather was better. She hadn't been to town either since we came here. Only Papa made the trip for supplies, coal and seed. But now that the snow was gone and the plowing and planting done, maybe we would go to town. When we did I would look for that little patch of trees.

But soon there was no time for anything but weeding and watering and hoeing. Papa had planted a big vegetable garden and built a fence around it. Each row seemed a mile long. It took all our spare time, even Mama's, to keep it weeded and watered. We took turns pumping and carrying. Watching the plants get bigger and bigger was some reward, but that didn't seem like enough for all the aching backs and muscles we got.

A new house was going up down where the roads crossed in front of Aunt Hilda's house. From our kitchen window I could see loaded wagons pass. Papa said Mr. Miller and his two sons were living in a tent now, but when the house was finished Mrs. Miller would come on from a place called Des Moines. I hoped they would be as nice neighbors as Uncle Ethan and Aunt Hilda. Most of all that the boys wouldn't be "smarties" like some boys were.

Several times that spring Papa took time to drive off somewhere in our biggest wagon and bring back a load of willow and cottonwood cuttings. The nearest natural timber, he said, was a patch near the river about twenty miles from Stebbinsville. A farmer who had settled there was doing a nice business selling cuttings to new settlers.

"He gets a good price for 'em but I guess they're worth it. They grow fast and strong and we're going to need a strong windbreak."

Papa talked a lot about the winds on the Iowa prairies. He said they could sweep away everything in their path, even houses and barns and animals; and that without a good strong windbreak in winter the snow could bury houses and barns in a few hours. I looked at the little willow and cottonwood cuttings and wondered how they could ever grow strong enough to keep wind and snow from destroying us. We were all glad Papa was going to build that windbreak.

As usual, all of us helped to build the windbreak. Papa dug holes and planted the new trees. Elsie and Vina and I carried water to them from the big tank — an added daily task until the trees were well-rooted. They grew fast, soon making a low green wall to the north of our house. Papa went for more cuttings, this time for other purposes. He brought back box elder, ash, hickory and walnut cuttings, and two catalpas Mama wanted very much. The box elder was planted at each side of the front walk, and two ash trees in the front yard to shade the porch. Mama insisted on planting the catalpas herself — one on each side of the downstairs bedroom window. One cottonwood was put in the back yard, another at the south side of the house. With hickory and walnut cuttings, Papa started a small grove northeast of the house, and marked off a big patch of ground northwest of the house for an orchard. On his next trip for cuttings he bought mulberry and plum, apple and cherry.

Aunt Hilda and Uncle Ethan had been too busy with their own plowing and planting to do much visiting lately. But when all the trees were in, Mama invited them to supper and to show them how much our farm had changed.

"Sam Bullard, you're the hardest working man I ever saw," Uncle Ethan exclaimed as Papa showed them around the grounds. "It's a regular Garden of Eden!"

Papa was in a generous mood that evening. "Don't give me all the credit. Molly and the kids helped."

"*Ja!*" Aunt Hilda's eyes twinkled. "Vat good *kinder* to farmer!"

Even Papa laughed this time. He and Aunt Hilda were good friends now, but she still could give him a "tongue lashing" in that funny language if she thought he deserved it. It was one of the happiest evenings we had had at the farm.

When they had gone we sat on the front porch listening to the night sounds and counting the stars as they came out. The sky looked like dark blue velvet and the wind was gentle as thistledown.

"It's hard to believe this is the same place we came to in February," Mama said.

"It sure is. But I told you this is good soil, Molly. And just you wait 'til those trees start climbing toward the sky! Then you'll really see a Garden of Eden right here on the prairie. Why, before you know it we'll be having apple and cherry pies from our own trees. And all the plum butter I can eat!"

Mama laughed softly. "That will take a while I'm afraid." Then she added, "It *is* good land, Sam. Real good."

65

CHAPTER VI
1890

We were soon to learn the Iowa prairie was not always a Garden of Eden. Thunderstorms that summer were just awful! Mama and Papa didn't seem to mind them but Elsie and Vina and I would cover our heads at the first flash of lightning and wait in terror for the crash of thunder. If it came quickly and loud we knew it was close by. If it was a while before thunder rumbled, it was far enough away not to harm us.

One hot, sticky July day there were flashes of heat lightning off and on all afternoon. The skies rumbled like potatoes poured onto a wagon bed. The air pressed down, motionless. The cottonwood leaves hung limp. And there wasn't even a whisper among the willows.

Lucy, playing near where I was weeding the turnip patch, lay down in the grass and went to sleep. When I finished the row I picked her up and took her to the house. Mama was canning tomatoes. Vina was putting the filled jars in neat rows on the butttery shelf. Mama looked up.

"Did you finish the weeding?"

"Almost. It was so hot and Lucy got sleepy."

"Better put her on the downstairs bed. Looks like a storm's brewing."

I sat on the bed beside Lucy, more frightened than I wanted to admit. After a while I went to the dining-room window. The sun looked strange. It was dull yellow and there was a big black cloud behind it like it was going to swallow everything.

Then suddenly the wind came, lashing the cottonwoods and willows. Darkness settled over the windbreak. The skies opened with a downpour. Through thick sheets of rain I could barely see Elsie and Papa running toward the wagon down in the grain field. Lightning flashed, instantly followed by a crash of thunder. It shook the house. I ran to the kitchen. Mama and Vina were closing windows and doors. "See about the upstairs windows, Ann," Mama called.

Upstairs the wind seemed stronger, whipping through the

66

house. I got the windows closed and pressed my face against the back one trying to see Papa and Elsie. I couldn't see a thing. Suddenly the beams above my head cracked and groaned. I screamed and ran downstairs.

"Get Lucy!" Mama shouted above the pounding rain. She snatched the oil-cloth off the table and wrapped it around little Mae. She was wrapping Lucy in Papa's old denim jacket when he burst into the house.

"Quick! To the soddy! It's a cyclone." He took Lucy and Mama carried Mae. Fighting wind and rain we finally reached the soddy. It was dry, and Elsie was there. Mama quieted Mae and Elsie took charge of Lucy. Vina and I stood, dripping, in the center of the room. We had other things to fear now besides the dark back room. Papa walked about muttering, "I *knew* that storm cellar should have been finished! But how can a man be in ten places at once?"

"We'll be all right here," Mama said.

"I just hope the house is," he grumbled.

What if it wasn't! Would we have to live here in the soddy until Papa built a new house? I looked toward the back room and shivered.

For a long time no one spoke. Outside the wind howled like the world was coming to an end. Through the tiny window we could see steady flashes of lightning. Would it never stop! Suddenly there was a blinding flash and crash of thunder. The earth trembled.

"That was a close one," Papa said, and paced the room.

I held my breath. Surely the next crash would destroy us all. It did not come. The wind seemed to die down. Inside the soddy it was now dark as night. It was scary to hear voices and not see the speaker.

"It seems to be letting up," Papa said. He opened the soddy door. It was still raining and thunder rumbled in the distance. Then above the sound of rain and thunder we heard the hooves of galloping horses and shouting voices.

Papa ran outside. A second later he yelled, "Fire! The house is on fire! Leave the kids and hurry!"

Elsie took the baby. Mama vanished in the darkness. Lucy and Vina and I huddled in the doorway but the soddy faced away from the house so we couldn't see anything. We could only wait. After a few minutes of that I could stand it no longer. I had to know what was happening. "Stay here, Vina." I started out.

Elsie yelled, "Come back! Do you want to drown?"

"I can't get any wetter," I told her and stepped outside where I could see.

Flames were shooting up into the sky. The whole roof of the house was burning. Mama was pumping water. The neighbors had formed a bucket-brigade. Papa was up on the ladder emptying the buckets on the roof. Thick smoke billowed up and the rain beat it back to earth. It was like some terrible dream.

I went back inside. "Oh, it's awful! Just awful! The whole house is on fire!" I was crying and couldn't stop.

Pretty soon the smoke began to seep into the soddy. Vina and Lucy started coughing. Elsie, with Mae in her arms, closed the door. "Stop bawling, Ann! *That* won't put out the fire."

I put my hand over my mouth and sat down. We could still hear the shouting outside. After a few endless minutes, Elsie couldn't stand it either. She gave Mae to Vina and both of us went outside. Nothing had changed. Mama was still pumping water. The brigade passed the buckets to Papa on the ladder. Suddenly he yelled, "Hold it!" and disappeared in a smoke cloud. Pretty soon we could see him ripping steaming shingles from the edge of the roof. Then like answer to a prayer, it started to rain again. The flames died down and finally flickered out..

Papa came down the ladder and joined the others, shouting, "We've got to save the furniture!"

Now Elsie and I could help. We ran through the driving rain to the house. Part of the roof had been saved. By lantern light Mama and Papa and the neighbors began carrying the furniture into the protected part. Elsie and I grabbed anything we could carry. Mama and Aunt Hilda worked with the men, getting the heavy stuff out. By the time the work was done the rain had stopped. Mama looked at Elsie and me as if we were strangers.

"What are you kids doing here? Where's Vina and Lucy and Mae?"

"They're all right in the soddy. We wanted to help," Elsie said.

Mama looked awfully tired. Her clothes were soaked and her face streaked with soot and mud. She picked up one of the lanterns and started toward the soddy. We followed. Inside she leaned against the wall and put her hand over her heart. She acted like she couldn't get her breath, and she paid no attention to Mae and Lucy who ran to her, crying. Suddenly she closed her eyes and crumpled to the floor. Elsie screamed. I ran as fast as I could to get Papa.

Mama was coming to when Papa and Aunt Hilda got there. Aunt Hilda said something in German. Papa picked up Mama and started toward the house, calling, "Bring the kids, Hilda!"

We spent the night with Uncle Ethan and Aunt Hilda. In the next room Mama lay with her eyes closed, scarcely breathing. "If Mama dies," Elsie sobbed, "I'll . . . I'll run away . . . back to Illinois!"

"Don't say that!" I was trying not to cry but I felt as she did. We couldn't stay here without Mama.

Aunt Hilda must have heard us. "Your mama get well, *kinder*. Now, to sleep you go!"

Alvina propped herself up on one elbow. "Let's sing Mama's song."

"Is *goot*," Aunt Hilda agreed. She blew out the lamp and left us alone.

Vina started to sing. She was asleep before she reached the chorus. Elsie's sobs gradually faded away, too. I lay awake thinking about Mama and our house. Aunt Hilda had said Mama would get well. It must be true. She wouldn't tell a fib. But the house—would Papa rebuild it, or would we have to live in that scary old soddy after all? I must have gone to sleep thinking about that because I dreamed the wind was blowing me like a kite and the sky was filled with flames. Mama was pumping water and Papa was trying to reach the fire but the ladder wasn't long enough. He kept calling to me to come down. Then the wind stopped and I began to fall down . . down . . . down.

Aunt Hilda had breakfast ready when we tiptoed into the kitchen the next morning. "Come, *kinder*, pancakes I make."

69

She lifted Lucy into a chair made higher with pillows. Mae was still asleep. We took our places at the table. Papa and Uncle Ethan weren't there. I guessed they had gone to our house.

"May we see Mama first?" I asked.

"Later you see. Breakfast now you eat."

When Aunt Hilda opened the door to Mama's room we tip-toed to the side of the bed. Her eyes were closed. Her face was as white as the pillow-slip. "Is she . . . dead?" Vina whispered.

"Ssssh!" Aunt Hilda shook her head and shooed us quietly out of the room and closed the door. "She *joost* tired. Ve let her sleep now."

We sat in the kitchen and waited. After a while Papa came. He *had* been to the house. "It's pretty bad, but I guess we can save something." He spoke to Elsie. "You and Ann come and help get the place cleaned up. Vina can look after Lucy and the baby." He turned to Aunt Hilda. "How is she?"

"How you t'ink!" she snapped. "The *goot* God you should be thanking she not in her grave already!"

Papa looked glum and stalked out. We had to go, too, but neither of us wanted to leave without seeing Mama. Aunt Hilda promised we could see her when we came back for lunch, so we followed Papa.

The upper part of the house was almost all burned away. Only black, water-soaked stumps stood where once there had been walls papered with yellow-flowered paper. Some of the roof remained but we could see the skies through holes in it. The upstairs floor hadn't burned through so had given some protection to the furniture we'd moved last night. All morning Elsie and I, Papa and Uncle Ethan, carried mattresses and bed clothing into the yard and spread them to dry. The skies had cleared and the sun, after the storm, was quite warm. A soft wind blew from the east. Scrubbing soot from the downstairs walls which still stood was an endless dirty task.

"Why didn't all of it burn?" Elsie complained. "We could build a new house in less time than it'll take us to make what's left of this decent."

When we returned to Aunt Hilda's at noon Mama was awake. We were allowed to see her, but only for a few minutes.

70

She smiled weakly as we gathered about the bed. Lucy began to cry. "Now, now!" she said softly. "I'll be all right, girls. Just be good and do what Aunt Hilda says."

"Aunt Hilda say come eat. Let mama rest."

As the days passed we began to understand that Mama wasn't going to be all right "in a few days" as she and Aunt Hilda had promised. She lay, still and white, in the darkened room and nothing anyone did made her better. As soon as our house was fit to live in again Papa wanted to move her back to it.

"You've got your own work to do, Hilda. The girls can look after Molly."

Aunt Hilda's hands went to her hips, always a sign she was angry. "Here Molly stay, Sam Bullard! You bring doctor!"

Mama and baby Mae stayed at Aunt Hilda's but Papa did nothing about a doctor.

Two more weeks went by. Even Aunt Hilda admitted Mama was worse. Sometimes when I went to see her I thought she didn't want to get well. Still Papa did nothing about getting a doctor. Finally Uncle Ethan went to town and brought one back. All of us waited in the kitchen while the doctor was with Mama. It seemed a long time before he came out and spoke to Papa.

"Your wife's a mighty sick woman, Mr. Bullard. Why didn't you come for me sooner? I'll do what I can now but it may not be enough. She's completely exhausted. That storm and the fire, so soon after having the baby, were too hard on her."

Papa said nothing. We waited. Did "the last straw" mean Mama would never get well? The doctor went on talking to him. "Let me tell you, Mr. Bullard, this is a rough life for any woman. Don't make it any rougher than necessary. And that is apparently just what you have done. She needs rest now, a lot of rest. And some place away from here where there's too many reminders of tragedy." He picked up his hat and bag. "That's my advice. And if you want to keep your wife alive you'd better do something soon."

Papa waited until the doctor had left before he exploded. "Doctors! They're all alike! Molly can rest at home as well as any place. Maybe better. He talks like the cyclone and fire were my doing. And having children never hurt any woman. That's her job, the way God intended."

Aunt Hilda had heard enough. Now she exploded. "You *dummkopf*. If Molly die what you do then, Sam Bullard?"

"She's not going to die. Molly's a strong woman. She has to get well. A man can't bring up a family of girls out here without a woman."

Aunt Hilda started to say something, then closed her lips tight and glared at him a second before she left him sitting there and went into Mama's room.

Elsie and Vina and I looked at each other. I knew we were thinking the same thing. Mama might die! Even the doctor had said as much. But she *mustn't!* We couldn't *live* without Mama. If God wanted someone to die, why couldn't it be Papa? Then all of us could go back to Grandma and Grandpa. Oh, it was so unfair! And I hated Papa more than ever.

That night when the others were asleep I got up and went outside. It was clear and warm. The sky glowed with millions of stars. Surely, I thought, Jesus must be very close. If I prayed real hard He would hear me. I closed my eyes.

"Dear Jesus, *please* let Mama get well and please, oh, please let us go back to Grandma's!"

I knew I should also ask Him to forgive me for hating Papa. Mama said just asking was not enough; we must be sorry for our sins *before* we asked forgiveness. But hard as I tried I just couldn't be sorry about hating Papa.

I guess Jesus understood. He answered my prayer anyway. When Uncle Ethan came back from town a few days later he brought two letters. One from Grandma and the other from Uncle Phil. Papa and Elsie were in the fields and Vina was down in the orchard with Lucy. I looked at the letters again then climbed into his buggy.

Aunt Hilda went into Mama's room first to see if she was awake. I kissed Mama then held out the letters. "They're from Grandma and Uncle Phil."

Mama didn't reach for them but her eyes opened wider and smiled a little. "Let Aunt Hilda read them to me." She tried to sit up, then lay back on the pillow.

Aunt Hilda opened Grandma's letter first and read: "Dear Molly and Sam. It is a long time since our last letter. We hope you are all well and that the Lord grants you a good harvest. From the sound of your last letter I know you have earned it.

"Molly, your father hasn't felt very well for some time. He wants so much to see you and the children and so do I. If you and the girls can get away for a week or so this fall we'll send you the money to come for a visit. Maybe Sam can come too when the crops are harvested, but if he can't we'll understand. Do try to come, Molly. We miss all of you so much. And write soon. Love to all."

"Oh, Mama, do you think we *could* go?"

"We'll see, honey." That meant she had to ask Papa, and there'd be no visit.

"This for Sam, Molly. You want I open?" Aunt Hilda held up the other letter.

"No, save it for him. He can read it to me tonight." She took Grandma's letter and held it lovingly. Uncle Phil's letter lay on the table beside her bed.

I told Elsie and Vina about the letters when I got home but I didn't mention them to Papa. Maybe, just maybe, Mama wouldn't tell him about Grandma's letter. Maybe she'd hurry up and get well and we'd go without asking him. But I knew that was only silly hope. Mama would never do anything against Papa's wishes. We were eager, though, to hear what was in Uncle Phil's letter and hurried supper and the dish washing.

But Papa *didn't* read the letter out loud! Not even to Mama. He just read it silently, folded it and put it in his pocket. We waited. Mama glanced at him several times, waiting too, before she asked, "Did Phil say anything about the crops there this summer?"

"No. But they musta been good. He painted the house. Says he had to trim those catalpa trees to keep the leaves out of the paint."

Mama smiled. "They should be in bloom now. Such a beautiful sight!"

After a while Papa said, "Elmer's getting restless I guess. Phil says he's thinking about taking a quarter section of land out here. Says if he does he'll have to get rid of the farm we sold him. Can't manage it without Elmer."

73

Mama didn't reply at once. When she did her voice seemed stronger and a little excited. "Sam, why don't you trade him this farm for our old one?"

"Now don't start that kind of talk again, Molly," Papa snorted. "I'm *not* going to sell this farm." Then he saw Grandma's letter on the table. "Are your folks all right?"

"Read it for yourself." She sighed and closed her eyes.

He read the letter, refolded it and put it back on the table. "Too bad about your father." We waited for him to go on but he didn't. Not one word about Grandma's invitation. Pretty soon he stood up. "We better be getting on back. There's work to do. Come along, kids." He leaned and touched his lips to Mama's forehead. "Hurry up and get well, Molly. We need you."

After that visit Mama suddenly began to get better. I wondered if it was because of Grandma's letter or Papa's needing her. Maybe she thought she *could* get Papa to let us go. Each time we were permitted to see her I wanted to ask her about this but I didn't. It might upset her. Her voice was stronger now and she smiled a lot the way she used to. Some days when we arrived she was sitting up in bed and her cheeks were pink.

Several days passed. I could not stand the wondering any longer. I decided to go to see Mama alone. Maybe if the others weren't there she'd tell me what she was going to do about the letter and the visit to Grandma.

I waited until Elsie and Papa had gone back to the field after lunch and Lucy was taking a nap. I told Vina about my plan and asked her to make excuses for me if Papa missed me before I got back.

"All right. But hurry. He'll tan your hide good if he finds out."

I ran all the way to Aunt Hilda's. Mama hugged and kissed me and asked if something was wrong; shouldn't I be working in the garden this time of day. I clung to her. "No. No. I just had to see you, Mama. You *are* going to get well, aren't you? And we *will* go to see Grandma and Grandpa."

She held me close for a while before she answered. "Of course I'm going to get well, darling. I'm getting better every day. And I'll be back home before you know it. Then we'll see about going to Grandma's. Now run along, dear, and we'll all have a nice visit tonight." I kissed her goodbye and started out. "And Ann, maybe we'd better not mention this visit to the others."

"Thank you, Mama."

"If Aunt Hilda's in the kitchen, would you ask her to bring me a pencil and some paper? I think I feel well enough to-day to write to Grandma, let her know we got her letter and that we're all right."

"I sure will, Mama! I sure will!"

Mama never told any of us what she had written. But the strange thing was that she didn't give the letter to Papa or Uncle Ethan to mail. She kept it under her pillow! I supposed she was waiting to ask Papa about the visit. But several days later, when Aunt Hilda fixed Mama's pillows, the letter was still there.

At last she was well enough to be moved back to our house. Elsie and Vina and I worked all that morning to make sure the house was clean and orderly. Even Papa was kinder that day. Right after lunch he drove to Aunt Hilda's in the spring-wagon to bring Mama home. Aunt Hilda came along to carry Mae. She insisted Mama stay in bed the rest of the day and "laid down the law" to Papa.

"Molly still need plenty of rest, Sam. Joost you remember that!" She shook her finger in Papa's face. He didn't get angry. He *smiled* at her. He must be happy to have Mama home! Maybe, when she was stronger, he would let us go to Grandma's.

Mama was up and down, in and out of bed, for the next two weeks. She insisted upon helping as much as she could with the housework.

"You're supposed to rest, Mama," Vina told her. "For the trip to Grandma's."

Mama smiled. "How can I get my strength back if I don't use it?" She went on snapping green-beans for supper.

"Sure, silly!" Elsie put in, "And what makes you think we're going to Grandma's? Papa hasn't said so yet." She hurried out, slamming the door just hard enough to show how she felt.

"We are *too* going to Grandma's, aren't we Mama?" Vina pleaded.

"We'll see," she said. She put her hand in her apron pocket where she carried the letter she had written to Grandma. She didn't know I'd seen it when she put the apron on. Why hadn't she mailed it?

The room where Elsie and I slept was over the kitchen. When Papa rebuilt after the fire he cut a hole in the kitchen ceiling so the range heat would also heat our room. It was fine in winter, but not so nice in summer if Mama was baking and had the range going full blast for a long time. The foot-square opening was covered on both sides with a piece of wire mesh. Papa called this a "register". We couldn't see through it down into the kitchen, but we could hear conversations clearly. We also were careful to whisper if we didn't want what we were saying heard in the kitchen below.

That night we were sure Mama would talk to Papa about the trip to Roanoke. For once we didn't protest going to bed early. Upstairs, the three of us gathered in our room and hovered over the register. Papa was still sitting at the table. We could hear the creak of his chair every time he moved. Mama must have been fixing him more coffee. We could hear her footsteps on the bare floor, walking back and forth.

"I'll have another piece of that pie if there's any left," Papa said.

For a while things were quiet. Then Mama said, "Sam, I'm going to have to know pretty soon how to answer Mother's letter." We held our breath.

Papa took his time about answering. "I don't think you're in any condition to travel yet, Molly."

"But it will take a week or more for the letter to reach Roanoke and get Mama's reply back with the money for the trip. And in a couple of weeks . . . ."

". . . . you'll be cooking for threshers," Papa interrupted.

"But after that? Couldn't you get along without me and the children for a couple of weeks?"

"I've *been* getting along without a wife for a lot longer than a couple of weeks already."

Mama didn't say anything. Pretty soon we could hear her moving about making things to do the way she always did

76

when Papa was like this. Finally she said, "Have you forgotten what the doctor told you, Sam?

"What are you talking about?"

"He said if you wanted to keep me around I'd have to have a complete rest and change. You *do* want to keep me around don't you, Sam?"

"What kind of a fool question is that? I can't think of a surer way *to* lose you than letting you go back to Roanoke. First thing I know you'll be in Saunemin—with Phil."

"Don't be ridiculous! Mother says father isn't very well and I *would* like to see him. As for Phil . . . well, now who's being foolish? And by the way, have you answered his letter yet?"

"No."

"You should have, Sam. What are you going to tell him about the farm?"

"I don't know. What do you think I should tell him?"

That was a good sign! Maybe Papa would agree to trade this farm for our old one. Maybe Papa *was* going to do it! If he hadn't been thinking about it at least, he would have written Uncle Phil right away.

He didn't wait to hear Mama's opinion. "Shall I tell him how hard a man has to work to get a farm fenced and crops in? How long it takes to get a good windbreak started before a cyclone comes along and blows everything away? And how lucky *he'd* be to get a farm with all that done? Should I encourage his boy to come on out here, or stay in Illinois where life is easy?"

We sat back on our heels and looked at each other. What had gotten into Papa? We'd never heard him talk this way before. Maybe he *had* had enough of pioneering!

Mama was speaking again. We leaned close to the register. "Just be honest with him, Sam. Put the good and the bad down side by side. Tell him it's a wonderful place to make a living . . . unless he also wants a life *worth* living."

"Now what in tarnation do you mean by that?"

"Simply that no life is worth living, Sam, if it doesn't provide more than food and shelter. Growing children need schools and churches, music, books and friends. We need those things too."

"Hilda seems to be doing all right without them. She understands what pioneering is. And it takes that to open up a new part of the country. You're too impatient, Molly. We'll have all those things you talk about in time."

Again it was quiet for a while. Finally Mama said, "Very well, Sam. Write Phil whatever you want to write him. But now I have to know what to tell my folks. It's been almost three weeks since Mama's letter came."

"Make your own decision. Then if anything goes wrong you won't blame me. One thing, though. The older kids aren't going. I need them here to help get the corn in and take care of the house."

Mama gasped. "Sam, you can't mean that! The girls would be heartbroken. I couldn't go without them."

"Then that settles it. The girls *aren't* going. Now let's get to bed before I meet myself getting up."

We crept back to our beds.

"I told you Papa wouldn't let us go," Elsie whispered.

"But you heard what he said about how hard farming is here. Maybe he intends to trade the farm to Phil and we can all move back to Saunemin."

"In a pig's eye!"

I didn't really believe what I'd said. But it was better to think about that instead of Papa's last words. I couldn't bear to think we'd *never* see Grandma and Grandpa again.

Elsie was still asleep when I got up the next morning. So were Vina and Lucy when I peeked in. I dressed and went downstairs but I didn't go into the kitchen. I could hear someone moving around and it might be Papa. I didn't want to see him.

Then he spoke. "I don't know what you're sulking about, Molly. I told you you could go to Roanoke."

"You know I won't go without the girls."

"Suit yourself about that. I need Elsie and Ann here."

After a while Mama said, "What are you going to tell Phil about the farm?"

"If you must know, I'm going to tell him I have an option on that quarter section bordering ours on the east. Elmer can buy that if he wants to. I'd be proud to have him for a neighbor. But if he doesn't want it I'll buy it."

"What's going to happen to the old farm if Elmer comes out here?"

"That's nothing we have to worry about. Phil can do what he wants with it."

I waited in the sitting-room until Papa left then went into the kitchen. Mama was standing at the stove, her back to me. She was wiping her eyes with the corner of her apron. Pretty soon she lifted the stove lid and took Grandma's letter and her answer from her apron pocket and dropped them onto the flaming coals. For a moment she stood there, watching her dream go up in smoke. Then she replaced the lid and squared her shoulders and turned. And saw me standing in the doorway.

"I didn't hear you come down, child. Are the others up too? I was just going to call you."

I couldn't pretend. I ran to her and threw my arms about her waist, sobbing. Our last hope was gone. Mama knelt down and held me close. "Don't cry, darling. It's going to be all right. When the crops are in and I'm stronger Papa will see things differently."

I knew she was only trying to comfort me. Papa would never change his mind. If she hadn't known that she wouldn't have burned the letters.

CHAPTER VII
1890

While Elsie and Vina washed the dishes the next morning, I made beds and swept the floors. Mama sat at the kitchen table writing another letter to Grandma. All of us had outside chores to do but none of us wanted to leave the house until we knew what Mama wrote to Grandma. She didn't scold us for dawdling. When she finished the letter and looked it over, she called us together and read it aloud.

Dear Mama: Your letter arrived over two weeks ago and you must be wondering why I haven't answered it. The truth is I have been sick. In July we had a bad storm. Our house was struck by lightning and badly damaged. Fortunately all of us had taken shelter in the old soddy or we might have been killed. Sam rebuilt the house but the strain of fighting the fire and lifting so much put me in bed for a while. I'm up and around again now and beginning to get my strength back, so you must not worry about me or the children.

It would be wonderful to see you and Papa, but I am afraid we can't make the trip now. Sam needs us here. I'll have threshers to cook for in a week or two as soon as we can get the rig and crew. We are thankful the crop has been good. By then the corn will be ready to harvest, and when that is done there's the butchering and other fall work. And in October school starts. We haven't a schoolhouse as yet, but Hilda Stone, who is the best neighbor anyone ever had, is letting us use her dining room until we can get one built. We have a part-time teacher from Stebbinsville. Next year we hope to have our own teacher and a school-house, and maybe a Church. And Sam is talking about building two more rooms onto our house next spring when the crops are in. I'd like to get some rugs and curtains made this winter.

I pray Papa is feeling much better. I wish with all my heart we could come to you now, but it doesn't seem right to leave Sam with so much work to do. The children send their love. They are well but very disappointed we can't come. Maybe we can all come next summer. God bless you both. Love. Molly.

She put the letter down. No one said anything for a while. Elsie broke the silence. "Oh, Mama, why? *Why* is Papa so mean? He *never* lets us go any place. Just work, work, work!"

"You mustn't talk that way, Elsie. Papa does what he feels is best for all of us." She spoke softly in a choked voice.

"Best for the *farm!* He doesn't care two pins about us."

This time Mama spoke sternly. "That will be enough, young lady! You are old enough to know better. I may not always agree with Papa, but he is your father and he does care about all of us. I want to visit Grandma and Grandpa as much as you girls do, but we can't go this fall, so I don't want to hear any more about it." Her voice softened. "Now run along, all of you, and do your chores."

Elsie put on her sunbonnet and went out. The screen door slammed. I grabbed my bonnet and followed. "You shouldn't have talked that way to Mama. You know as well as I do *why* she isn't going to Grandma's. *She* could go, but she won't go without us. I think we ought to try to make things easier for her."

"Look who's being noble!" Elsie snapped.

"I'm not trying to be noble. I *am* trying to think of Mama instead of myself, and it wouldn't hurt you to do the same."

"Oh, go chase a grasshopper!" She ran off toward the field where Papa was stacking grain for threshing. Poor Elsie! I knew how hurt she was. She didn't really mean all the things she said sometimes. Most of the time I think she was madder at herself than anyone else.

Mama had said she didn't want to hear any more about the trip to Roanoke. None of us mentioned it again. But somehow everything was suddenly different. Maybe it was because we no longer hoped. Until now, I think all of us had hoped Papa would get tired of pioneering and take us back to Saunemin. But he'd had a chance to buy back our farm and turned it down. The Iowa prairie was going to be our home forever. At least until Papa got tired of this place and took a notion to "pioneer" in some other undeveloped wilderness. Mama's hard work and ours wouldn't count at all. He'd just tell Mama to pack and she'd have to do it. And go wherever he wanted to.

One morning a few days after the letter to Grandma had been mailed, I awakened very early. I got up quietly and dressed and slipped outside into the cool dawn. There were still night shadows around the barn and corral, but the open fields were beginning to light up. Far away on the horizon the soft pink light of a new day faintly stained a cloudless sky. Nearby the grass glistened with dew. Thousands of silver-green leaves on the young cottonwood shimmered in the soft breeze.

A brand new beautiful day! And for the first time I think I really *saw* how beautiful the prairie could be. I stood there a long time. A rooster crowed, and pretty soon I could hear the cows stirring and mooing softly. When I turned to go inside I looked back. The stacks of grain in the field were suddenly bathed in morning sunlight. From where I stood they seemed to have turned to gold.

For days I thought about the beauty of that morning. It had been there many times before. I'd seen the sun rise before. But never had I seen things in quite the same way. Was it because I hadn't looked hard enough? Or that I'd been too busy hating Papa, or wishing we could go back to Saunemin, to see beauty in anything. Right then, before I went inside, I made up my mind to look for the good and beautiful in every new day. I knew it wouldn't always be easy. Especially when the work was hard and the weather bad — hot or cold. But maybe trying to see good in that would keep me from thinking how hard it was.

I didn't tell anyone about my resolution. But I think Mama must have "read my mind" because that night when she read to us from her Bible after supper, she chose a passage that said all of it. *Whatsoever things are pure, whatsoever things are lovely, whatsoever things are of good report .. think on these things.*

But it took me a longer time to understand what I guess Mama had known all the time. That here on the Iowa prairie we must find happiness or lose it altogether.

Soon, too soon, it was threshing time. A time of hard work for everyone, but also a time for feasting. Neighbors came from their farms to help Papa with the big machines and wagons. Aunt Hilda came to help Mama, and Vina and I helped them.

There seemed no end to cooking and washing dishes. Besides the three regular meals each day, the threshing crew had to have a mid-morning and mid-afternoon "snack." And quite a "snack" it was!

Elsie was old enough to help in the fields. She and the two Miller boys took turns pitching bundles of cured grain into the thresher. Papa and one of the neighbors saw to it that the golden stream poured into the wagons and not onto the ground. It was a wonderful sight to watch. Sometimes, after I'd driven the cows to pasture, I went with Mama and Aunt Hilda when they took the mid-morning snack to threshers. While they were setting out the lunch onto the endgate of one of the wagons, another wagon was filling up with plump, golden grain. When the whistle blew the men lost no time. They scrambled down from machines and wagons and filled their plates and sat down wherever there was shade.

What Mama and the men called "a snack" seemed to me a pretty hearty meal. Big granite pots of strong coffee, several dozen doughnuts, and poplar-chips which some folks called scones. The way the men ate I wondered how they could be hungry again at noon. But they were. Hot and dusty, they'd wash up in the tin basins Mama kept on a long bench just outside the kitchen door. She had made the table in the kitchen bigger with several "leaves," and every day it was loaded with platters of beefsteak and bowls of mashed potatoes and gravy, with plenty of bread and butter. Dessert was big slabs of fruit pies and more strong coffee. Vina and I stood at each end of the table waving freshly cut box-elder branches to keep the flies away.

Only after the men and Elsie had returned to the fields could we take time to eat. Including Mama and Aunt Hilda. Then by the time we'd finished washing the dishes it was time to take mid-afternoon snack to the workers. And by the time they got back it was time to start supper. As soon as supper was over and the men and Aunt Hilda had left, Vina and I washed the piles of dishes while Mama prepared for the next day of cooking. Papa and Elsie were already in their beds. They had to be up and ready for work again at daybreak. Mama had to be up before daybreak to have breakfast ready, but I guess no one ever thought about that.

Somehow all of us lived through "threshing time." On the last day which was Saturday, I went with Mama and Aunt Hilda to take the mid-morning snack. The men seemed to be enjoying their work today more than usual. They were joking among themselves as they tossed bundles of grain into the thresher and laughing like it was a game of horseshoes.

Mama remarked about this to Aunt Hilda. "They're up to something. I wonder what."

"Today they finish. They joost happy. Maybe a dance ve should do, too!"

Mama smiled. "You dance if you want to. I'm too tired."

The men gulped their coffee and doughnuts and went right back to work. No rest in the shade today. "What's got into them, Sam?" Mama asked.

"They're trying to finish by noon."

"But why? Ours is the last threshing job this season."

Papa didn't explain. He told Mama to be sure to have dinner ready at noon, and went back to the grain wagons.

Dinner *was* ready at noon. The threshing *was* finished. The men washed up and ate, clowning and joking between bites. Uncle Ethan was the first to leave the table.

"See you all at my house," he said and hurried out. Aunt Hilda called to him but if he heard he didn't let on.

"What's going on, Sam?" Mama asked.

"Nothing for you women to worry about. Did you press my blue suit?"

"Yes, but what's the . . .?"

Papa was already on his way to the bedroom and didn't answer. When he came out he was wearing his best suit, shirt and shoes and carrying his best hat. All dressed up on a Saturday afternoon! Why? He hurried out and climbed into the spring-wagon. Mama and Aunt Hilda looked after him. Aunt Hilda's hands went to her hips. *"Dummkopf!"*

That night Papa kept us waiting supper for him. The last time we'd had to wait supper had also changed our lives. Would that happen again? Giving up the farm in Saunemin had been hard enough. Now maybe we were going to have to give up this one and move again? If so, it wouldn't be to the old farm, that was sure!

When Papa finally came I thought how foolish I'd been.

84

He was in a very jolly mood. He picked Mama up and swung her around and hugged and kissed her.

"Sam Bullard! Have you been drinking?"

Papa laughed, then started clowning, acting like he *was* drunk. He didn't fool any of us, though. All of us knew Papa never drank whiskey. Finally he dropped into a chair by the table. "What a day, Molly! What a day!"

Mama didn't say anything. She warmed the meat and potatoes and brought them to the table. We sat there waiting for Papa to start eating so we could. He didn't. "The crops were good. The threshers worked hard. It called for a celebration," he said.

"So you celebrated. Now eat your supper, Sam. We've been waiting quite a while and the children are hungry."

Papa went right on talking as if he hadn't heard. ". . . so I took all the men to the circus. And what a time we had!"

Mama started to say something but must have changed her mind. She began filling our plates, not serving Papa first the way she usually did. "Eat your supper, girls." We ate and Papa talked.

"You should have seen those women on the trapeze, Molly. Pink tights and spangles . . . hanging by their knees or leaping from one swinging bar to another as easy as you please. It was something to see!"

"Surely that wasn't all the circus had to offer," Mama said. I couldn't tell whether she was angry or just teasing.

"You bet it wasn't!" He leaned on the table and looked at us girls. "There were clowns with big feet and baggy pants, elephant acts, trained dogs and ponies, and popcorn and peanuts and pink lemonade. *And* a wild-west show. What do you think of that?"

"What should they think?" Mama asked, and now I knew she was angry. "The girls and I, and Aunt Hilda, spent *our* afternoon washing dishes and scrubbing floors and getting the flies out of the house. *And* cooking supper for a man who is now too full of popcorn and peanuts and pink lemonade to eat it!"

"No sense getting all riled up about it," Papa said. "This is the first year Stebbinsville has had a real circus. But it won't be the last, you can bet on that. The ringmaster told me they'd be back next year."

85

"Can we go next year?" Vina asked.

"Maybe. Depends on how well you do your work 'til then."

But we had done our work well *this* year! Why were the men rewarded and not Mama and the rest of us? It wasn't fair. Were women supposed to work as hard as men without even a thank-you? Maybe it would have been better to be born a boy. All girls and women ever did was work hard and take care of babies. Why did God *let* it be like that?

The hard work of threshing time was soon forgotten. Now the corn was ready for harvesting. This was work Papa and the rest of us could do without the help of our neighbors. Remembering Papa's promise to take us to the circus next year, all of us pitched in eagerly. Even Lucy wanted to help. She was too little to be in the fields but Mama let her help with the dishes. Standing on a chair beside the kitchen sink, Lucy wiped knives and forks and spoons as Mama lifted them out of the rinse water.

Elsie and Vina and I were up early the morning corn-harvest was to start. By the time we finished breakfast Papa had the team harnessed and hitched to the wagon with the bang-boards in place. When we got to the cornfield we climbed down and walked along beside the tall stalks, picking the ripened ears and tossing them into the wagon. The team didn't need driving. The horses plodded along at an even pace keeping close so we didn't have to look where we were throwing the ears of corn. They didn't even jump when the ears hit the bang-boards and fell into the wagon bed. When it was full, we girls rested in the shade of tall stalks. Papa drove back to the barn and dumped the load into the corncrib. While he was gone we talked.

"Do you think he'll really take us to the circus next year?" I asked.

"He promised he would," Vina reminded us. "*If* we worked hard. And we will, won't we?"

"We *always* work hard," Elsie said. "And what good does it do?"

"But he promised!" Vina repeated. "Mama heard him. He *has* to keep his promise."

"Maybe. And if he does," Elsie told us, "I'm going to have a new dress and dance and have fun and forget all the work I had to do to get there."

"Do they dance at the circus? I mean people like us, not the show people?"

"I guess so. Anyway, I'm going to have fun!"

Harvesting corn was hard work. By the end of the day we were hot and dusty and tired. We washed up and ate our supper and went to bed early. We had to be up at dawn, ready to go through another day just like the last one. This went on for more than a week. Now the corncrib was full ready for husking.

That night at supper Papa said, "There's a lot of corn to be husked, Molly. I've been thinking about getting some of the neighbors in to help. Why don't we have a husking-bee? We'd get the job done faster and have fun doing it."

"Do you think they'd have time? They must be pretty busy with their own harvesting."

"I never heard of a farmer too busy to go to a dance or a party. They'll come. Don't worry about that. The women will see to it."

Mama smiled. "You may be right, Sam. When do you want to have it?"

"Sooner the better. Saturday, I guess. I'll ride over tomorrow morning and tell Ethan and Ben Miller about it. They can help spread the word to others. Unless I miss my guess it's going to be quite a shindig."

Papa didn't miss his guess.

I remembered the husking-bees at our farm in Saunemin when I was too little to join in the fun. This time would be different. We were big enough now to gather the corn. Surely we were big enough to share the celebration. The promised circus was a long way off.

All day Friday Mama and Aunt Hilda cooked and baked. We girls cleaned house, and set up long tables made from boards with a "saw-horse" at each end in the back yard. By noon on Saturday a dozen chickens had been fried and other last-minute foods were ready. A row of pies covered with dish-towels, had been cooling on a table by the window since early morning.

Shortly after one o'clock the neighbors began to arrive. Elsie and I started carrying the food to the tables, now covered with sheets and a few tablecloths; Mama refused to use her best linen. There were several big platters of fried chicken and bowls of potato salad, plenty of deviled eggs and dishes of pickled beets and cucumbers. Aunt Hilda had brought two crocksful of coleslaw and *schmeercase*. Lucy and Vina had been taking turns at the ice cream freezers all morning. There would be gallons of it for dessert with cake and pie.

Elsie had spent an hour last night putting her hair up on rag curlers. Now soft golden curls fell about her shoulders. I'd never seen her look so pretty, and so happy. She wanted to put on her new voile dress with the full skirt, but Mama said it wasn't proper dress for a husking-bee. She'd grumbled a while about it. What use having pretty clothes if you never got to wear them! "There's a time and place for pretty clothes," Mama told her. "Go put on your flowered calico. It's pretty *and* proper for this occasion."

Jed Miller must have thought so too. His eyes lighted up every time he looked at her.

Vina danced in and out of the house and everywhere showing off her new green checked gingham with a *very* full skirt. Her eyes never stopped dancing. She had filled out since we came to Iowa, chubby like a big doll. Her hair looked almost red in the sunlight. I don't think she really knew how pretty she was; just so full of fun and mischief she couldn't stop bouncing.

My own dress was blue-and-white checked gingham, and made from the same dress pattern as Vina's. Mama had braided my hair and wrapped the braids around my head and patted them when she had finished. "My little princess!" she'd called me. Usually she called me "her solemn little girl." I liked "princess" much better. But I guess I was solemn most of the time. There was so much to think about, so much to learn.

Uncle Ethan watched us carrying out the platters and bowls of food. "You're going to have your hands full, Sam, with such pretty daughters," he said. "First thing you know every young man in the county'll be comin' a-courtin'." He winked at Papa.

Elsie blushed and tossed her head so the curls bounced. She whirled about and hurried back to the house, pretending she hadn't heard a word Uncle Ethan said. I knew she had, and that *she* knew Jed Miller was watching her.

Mama and Aunt Hilda came out with pitchers of lemonade, and told everyone to "Gather 'round!" The feasting began.

88

"You must give me your recipe for this cole-slaw, Hilda," Mrs. Miller exclaimed. "I've never tasted *anything* so good!"

"I'll settle for more of that fried chicken and potato salad," Mrs. Hughes said. "What *do* you do to it, Molly? I make good potato salad but it never tastes like this." She was a plump, jolly woman. We all liked her almost as much as Aunt Hilda.

"I don't think it's any better than yours, Martha," Mama said. "It just *seems* to taste better when someone else makes it!"

Mama smiled and went on refilling plates, cutting pies and cakes, and pouring coffee. I wondered when she was going to sit down long enough to eat some of the food she'd spent hours preparing. Finally Aunt Hilda made her sit down and filled a plate and brought it to her.

When everyone had stuffed themselves, and the last spoonful of ice cream had been scraped from the freezer with much lip-smacking, Papa said, "Don't any of you get the idea all this good food was for nothing. I've got a whole crib full of corn over there to be husked."

"Aw, have a heart, Sam!" Uncle Ethan groaned. "We're too full to move."

Everyone laughed and started groaning. Papa pulled his watch from his pocket. "All right. One hour for digestion. Then we husk corn."

The men stretched out on the grass. Some of the women helped Mama carry the empty dishes to the kitchen. When Elsie and I offered to help, Mrs. Hughes said, "No, girls. We'll do it. You mustn't spoil those pretty dresses." We didn't insist.

The most exciting game during a husking-bee was to see who could find the most red or calico ears of corn. The first man, or boy, to find a red ear got the right to kiss the prettiest girl — or the girl he *thought* was the prettiest. But the girl had something to say about the kissing. It usually ended in a chase. If he caught her, somehow it always seemed to be behind a bush or a tree, so we never knew whether the girl had *really* let him kiss her.

When the husking began I glanced at Elsie. I knew she was hoping Jed would find the first red ear. And the way he ripped the husks off those ears of corn, so fast you could hardly see them, he must have had the same idea. I felt kinda sorry when he didn't win. Papa found the first red ear of corn. He held it up for all to see, then made straight for Mama and kissed her hard right in front of all the neighbors.

"Molly's still the prettiest girl in the county," he boasted. "And the best cook." Mama blushed and looked pleased. The men gave Papa an argument. I guess they had to! Still, they admitted Mama was "mighty pretty" and there was certainly nothing wrong with her cooking if today's feast was a sample.

It was beginning to get dark by the time the husking-bee broke up. The corncrib wasn't emptied but there would be a lot less for us girls to husk. It was time now for the dancing. Mr. Miller played the "fiddle" and Uncle Ethan pumped away on his accordion like he enjoyed every minute of it. Even the younger children joined in the square dances which kept up until almost ten o'clock. With all that exercise everyone was ready for more cake and coffee.

At last the party broke up. The last wagon pulled away from our gate. Mama and Papa stood in the front room doorway waving goodbye. "It was a good party, Molly. And we did right well with the husking," Papa said when they came into the kitchen where Elsie and I had started on the dishes. "Must have done half of it or more. Shouldn't take the girls more'n a few days to finish it up."

He took off his coat and hung it on the back of a chair and sat down at the table. "Any of that chocolate cake left, Molly? If there is I'll have another piece, and some coffee before we turn in."

"You'll have to settle for cocoanut cake," Mama said, shaking the coffee-pot to see if there was any left. ". . . and half a cup of coffee." She sat down at the table across from him.

"The corn yield was better than I expected," Papa said. "I tell you, Molly, this is the best land I've ever owned."

Mama looked too tired to care about good land and big crops. A soft bed would be more to her liking I thought. But tomorrow was Sunday. All of us could sleep an hour later. We went to bed, tired but happy.

CHAPTER VIII
1891-92

Before winter's first snowstorm Mama had made several big jars of hominy. Sweet corn was gathered and dried and hung in cloth bags in the barn loft. Potatoes, beets, carrots and turnips — the year's root crops — were dug. Pumpkins and cucumbers picked, cabbages and onions gathered and sorted. All of these, except cucumbers, were stored in the old soddy and covered with thick blankets of straw to prevent freezing. Most of the cucumbers became pickles of various kinds, and cabbages not solid enough for storing, were shredded for sauerkraut and packed between layers of salt in big stone jars.

Fall was also butchering time. Certainly there was nothing "beautiful" about it, but I supposed it was necessary. Mostly it was men's work, and once again neighbors came to help. I stopped my ears against the sounds of squealing pigs as they went to their death. Afterwards they were plunged into huge kettles of scalding water, and the awful scraping sound that followed as the bristles were being removed made me shiver. Why wasn't there another way to provide food for the long hard winters? It was awful knowing the little pigs I had fed and watched grow into big fat hogs had to die so that we could live. And somehow worse knowing that as soon as the weather was cold enough there would be more butchering. This time the little calves, now big enough for our winter beef.

When the hog-killing was over Mama's part of the work began. She made cake-sausages which Elsie and I packed in stone jars and stored in the buttery. Then came several big crocks of headcheese and pickled pig's feet and slabs of side meat preserved with salt. Leaner slabs, and the hams, were cured in a hastily built smokehouse. Later, when beef-butchering was over, Papa hung the carcasses there to freeze. And for several days the kitchen was filled with the good smell of mince-meat.

One morning as I drove the cows to pasture I heard the honking of wild geese flying southward. Winter was not far off.

That fall Papa at last finished the storm-cellar he'd been

working on when he had time. The night of the cyclone and fire he'd vowed he'd let everything else "go hang" until it was finished. But I suppose with so much else to do he'd forgotten about the vow, and none of us remembered it when Mama got sick.

It was close to the back porch with a door right under the dining-room window. I thought it looked more like a big mole-hill than a cellar, but it was deep enough for Papa to stand up straight in it. There were wooden steps going down, and benches inside. A ledge all the way around just below the roofline, was used for storing canned fruit. A lantern hung on a peg beside the door ready for use. Papa was very strict about it being filled with oil, the wick kept trimmed and the chimney clean.

As soon as it was finished we girls were allowed to explore its wonders. I thought the cellar would make a wonderful play-house — if we ever had time to play. But there was never much time for that when the weather was warm, and in winter the cellar would be too cold. But it was comforting to know it was there. We'd be safe from cyclones now — and we knew there would be more cyclones. But we'd never have to spend another dark night in the soddy.

About the middle of October Aunt Hilda's sitting-room became a schoolroom five days a week. The pupils came from nearby farms, ten of us that first day. Elsie, Vina and I. Jed and Will Miller. Nellie and Bob Hughes. The three Simpson children, Tom, Zeke and Hattie. As soon as we were seated — Aunt Hilda saw to that — the teacher took charge. Her name was Annabelle Swan. She looked very strict, and she wasn't the least bit pretty. She wore a white shirtwaist and a long black skirt. Her hair was twisted into a tight knot on top of her head. Some of the boys giggled, but stopped in a hurry when she looked sternly at them. But afterwards she smiled and was real pleasant.

She picked up a notebook and pencil from the table, then told us her name, as if we didn't already know it, and made a little speech about all of us working together to "make learning an exciting experience."

"We shall begin by your giving me your names and ages." She wrote them down as we gave them, then divided us into two groups. The older pupils, and the younger. Elsie, Jed, Nellie,

Tom and Zeke made up the first group. Vina, Will, Bob, Hattie and myself the other. We had no desks, except Aunt Hilda's dining table. The table divided the two groups, and Miss Swan took turns with each group. When it was time to recite the older boys and girls were heard first, then dismissed so they could get home in time to help with farm chores. But Elsie always waited for Vina and me. She was in no hurry to get home before we did.

Just before Thanksgiving I awoke one morning to find the ground covered with snow. Now I wouldn't have to take the cows to pasture before school! And during recess we could make snowmen and play snowball, and skate on it when it was hard enough.

Aunt Hilda's place was only about a mile from ours. Until the snow got real deep we walked to school, carrying our lunch in tin pails. But when it became deep and crusted Papa took us in the bobsled and picked us up in time to help with the chores.

We had Thanksgiving dinner with Aunt Hilda and Uncle Ethan. The table groaned with the good things she had prepared, and we groaned later because we'd eaten too much. Afterwards Uncle Ethan played the accordion and all of us sang. For a while everyone forgot about the long hours we had worked all year.

As winter deepened the snow was no longer fun. It was now something to be endured. Something to wade through to get to the barn and the out-house, and to be shoveled when the drifts got too high. Papa stretched a rope between house and barn which he said would give us something to hold onto in strong winds and blizzards. He said we'd have plenty of both before spring came.

Only a blizzard kept us from attending school. Elsie and I liked school but for different reasons. "Lessons are easier than pitching hay," she said, giggling. I loved books. I'd have read all night if Mama had let me, and I found learning *was* fun, as Miss Swan had said it would be. Vina would have been happy to skip school entirely, but she didn't mind it either. Maybe she felt as Elsie did, that school was better than farm chores, which even in blizzards had to be done. Vina and I helped with the milking and gathered the eggs and fed the pigs. But it was Elsie who helped Papa pitch hay down from the barn loft and clean out the stalls. I understood better now why she hated Papa and the farm, and swore she'd run away the first chance she got and never come back. She never talked that way when Mama or Papa could hear; only to me at night when we could whisper secrets and complaints. We'd settle into our deep straw-tick bed, still shivering, and stretch out to warm our feet on the hot flatirons Mama had wrapped and put there a while before.

"Where will you run to?" I asked, teeth still chattering.

"Some place where it's *warm,* and never any farm work to do. Virginia, maybe. I might even get a job in an office and learn how to use one of those new writing machines Uncle Phil told us about."

"You wouldn't!" I cried, forgetting to whisper.

Elsie put her hand over my mouth. "Do you want Mama to hear you?" she whispered. "Anyway, what's so bad about working in an office with men. I have to work in the fields with men, don't I?"

"It's not the same. Besides, if you run away you won't get to go to the circus next summer."

"Oh, pooh! I'll see lots of circuses. Bigger ones, too!"

After she was asleep I wondered if she really would run away. I didn't blame her for wanting to get away from Papa, but surely she wouldn't leave Mama and her sisters.

Hard as we worked, life was not all work. The long winter evenings in the warm kitchen when chores were done and supper was over and the dishes washed, were happy times. We girls gathered around the table with our school books. Mama knitted or mended, and Papa read the farm journal or the weekly newspaper. If we finished studying in time we were allowed to play a few games of dominoes or checkers before we braved the cold stairway and our chilly room.

Sometimes Papa brought a piece of harness into the kitchen to mend and oil. Mama didn't approve of this at all. She didn't tell him so, but her lips would get tight and her knitting needles click faster and faster. Then we knew she was "aggravated with Papa."

One night the oil can tipped over and made a big dark spot on Mama's clean floor. Mama was really aggravated. "Oh, Sam, look what you've done! Do you have to bring that smelly old harness in the house to fix it? It will take a week of scrubbing to get that spot out."

"Harness has to be fixed and oiled," Papa snorted. "Do you expect me to work in the barn in twenty-below weather?" He wiped up some of the oil with a rag and hung the harness on a nail behind the stove. Pretty soon he went to bed.

Mama put aside her knitting and brought a cup of corn meal and spread it on the greasy spot. It soaked up most of the oil but tomorrow she would scrub it anyway. Mama couldn't "abide" a messy kitchen.

Saturday nights were the best times. We were allowed to stay up later. After supper Vina or I would bring a bowl of apples from the buttery and Mama or Elsie popped corn. It was a feast to look forward to all week, and we made it last as long as possible. We'd peel the apples and save the peeling to eat last, munching popcorn with both. Mama read aloud to us from whatever book she had chosen for this special time. I could close my eyes and imagine I was one of the people in the book, and for days afterwards live in a kind of story book world no matter what I had to do about the house or farm.

Suddenly it was Christmas. Our first Christmas in Iowa.

The week before Papa had taken Mama to town with him. When they returned she hurried into their bedroom with some of the packages. We knew they were presents so we didn't ask questions. We had our own Christmas secrets. Each of us had made a present for Mama and Papa. They'd been finished since October and hidden away in our room. We had to make them early while it wasn't too cold upstairs.

A few days before Christmas we spent evenings after supper making decorations for the tree. "Where *do* Christmas trees come from out here, Mama?" Vina asked.

Mama smiled. "Maybe Santa Claus has one of his elves leave them in town."

"Oh, Mama! We know better than that!" Elsie said.

"I don't care *who* brings it as long as we have one," Vina insisted.

Satisfied that there would be a tree, we gathered about the kitchen table with a bowl of flour-paste and the colored paper we'd been saving all year. Elsie and I cut the paper into small strips and all of us fashioned the paper rings. When these were

95

done, we strung popcorn and red berries into long garlands to drape the tree. And the day before Christmas Mama made popcorn-balls.

On Christmas Eve Papa waited until Mae was asleep and Lucy tucked in her bed upstairs, then he put on his coat and went outside, and came back with a cedar tree. It wasn't very tall but it was bushy with lots of branches, and it smelled so Christmasy. He set it up near the window in the sitting room and he wouldn't tell us where it had come from. We didn't really care. We were so happy to have it. Long before midnight the tree was draped with our colored-paper chains and streamers. Mama dotted the branches with little balls of cotton-snow, and fastened a big silver star she had made to the top of the tree. Now it was time for our presents. They wouldn't be opened until tomorrow morning but we brought them from their hiding place and tucked them among the branches. Mama and Papa waited until we had gone to bed to put their presents under the tree.

Christmas morning was an exciting time. No one had to be called twice, even called at all. We were awake before daylight, waiting for the big moment. But no matter how early we ventured downstairs, Mama was up before we were and had breakfast ready. Only after we had eaten were we allowed to gather around the tree in the sitting room. It was hard to sit still, waiting for our turn, as the presents were distributed one by one.

"Did Santa Claus really bring the tree, Mama?" Lucy asked.

Vina didn't give Mama a chance to answer. "I know where it came from. I know!" She ran to Mama and whispered in her ear. Mama smiled. By then Lucy had forgotten her question and dumped her box of alphabet-blocks onto the floor with a clatter.

Christmas Day was also a time for feasting. Besides the good things Mama prepared for this special day, and the popcorn-balls we had only at Christmas, there were hard "ribbon" candy and bon-bons filled with coconut, and home-made taffy we had pulled for hours until it was like a long golden rope. When it cooled, we cracked it into chewy pieces and put it in a fruit jar. It would last long after Christmas.

Our presents were useful presents. Fascinators, stocking caps, mittens. Or books and pencil boxes and colored crayons. Our gifts to Mama and Papa were simple things we had made from scraps of material and bits of ribbon we had saved all year.

This special day passed all too quickly. Even on Christmas the chores had to be done. But none of us minded too much. There was Mama's special Christmas dinner to look forward to when we came in. And the long evening in the warm kitchen. We tried on the presents that could be worn several times, eager to show them off when we went back to school.

Mid-February a Chinook wind came. The deep snow disappeared quickly. But now we knew a Chinook wind brought a false spring. Winter and snow would return when the wind had blown itself out. For several days we plodded through deep slush to do the chores, and watched streams appear and flood the land. The mile-walk to school was worse than wading deep snow. We were almost glad when cold weather set in again. Picking our way over frozen, bumpy ground was easier than wading through slush.

Winter passed. Little patches of green once more appeared on the prairie. The ice on the watering tank was gone when we did morning and evening chores. Presently the patches of green spread until the whole prairie was a big green carpet. Warm winds rippled the fresh new grass. Soon flowers appeared after a long winter's sleep.

Spring was a wonderful time. It was also housecleaning time. The straw in all bed-ticks had to be replaced with clean, new straw. Carpets had to be taken up and carried outside and swept on both sides with a stiff broom. Then they were hung on the clothesline and beaten with sticks until all the dust was gone. Straw was also used as padding under the home-made rag carpets. This must be replaced with new straw and spread evenly before the carpets were put down again and fastened to the floor with hundreds of carpet tacks.

This dirty, back-breaking task fell mostly to Mama and Vina with Lucy holding tacks and hammer while the carpet was well stretched. I was now old enough to help Elsie and Papa with plowing and planting. And soon as that was finished, Elsie and Papa began the endless job of cultivating the corn. I followed the cultivator and pulled weeds it had missed. Vina joined me as soon as the carpets were down again.

Bending and stooping over the long rows was back-tiring work. Sometime I felt I would break in two if I bent over one more time, but I didn't slow down until I got to the end of the row. It helped to think about nice things, such as the circus next summer and maybe a visit to Grandma's.

The promised circus was always in our minds. At night, bone tired, Elsie and I lay in our bed, buried in the new straw tick which was so high we had to use a chair to climb up on it, and talked about the "big day." But even something as exciting to look forward to as the circus didn't keep us awake very long. We counted the days, and if we felt like complaining about the long hours and hard work, we choked back the words and endured what we had to.

That spring Uncle Phil's boy, Elmer, bought the quarter section east of our place. Some of the work Papa usually did now fell to us so that Papa could help Elmer get his crops in and a shack built. And when Elmer's crops *were* in, Papa spent more time at his place than ours, helping build the new house.

In June the doctor delivered a lusty baby boy to Aunt Hilda. They named him Hans Ethan. Now Mama spent a good deal of time at their place, so Elsie and I, and Vina part of the time, did all the chores at our place except the really heavy work which Papa did when he got home. He and Uncle Ethan were helping the Millers build a bigger barn. Sometimes I wondered why each farmer didn't just take care of his own place? But Mama often said how good it was that people out here helped each other because that made everyone a good neighbor; and in this new country good neighbors were very important. Like that night our house burned. Without the neighbors' help there wouldn't have been enough left *to* rebuild.

So most of the time we girls thought about the circus, and endured.

Toward the end of June Papa started adding two more rooms to our house — upstairs and downstairs bedrooms. Mama was very excited about this. Now she could have a parlor. The building went slowly because there was always so much other work to be done. So it was July before the addition was finished.

One evening we were all sitting outdoors under the big cottonwood after supper. It had been an unusually hot day and the house was stifling. Elsie and I lay on the grass, cooling off before we gave in to the heat of our bedroom. Vina chased fireflies. She never could sit still very long at a time, even in hot weather. Snatches of Mama's and Papa's conversation drifted through our own whispered talk. Suddenly Mama exclaimed, "Oh, my goodness, Sam! We forgot all about the schoolhouse!"

"Well, we got along all right last year without a schoolhouse."

"But Hilda has her baby now. We can't expect her to let us use her sitting room again this fall."

Papa said, teasing. "Ethan's responsible for the baby. Why not let him be responsible for the new schoolhouse?"

"Be serious, Sam! We can't do without some kind of school, not with so many new settlers and several more children."

Elsie whispered, "Papa's mad at Uncle Ethan because *he* got a boy baby."

I didn't hear what Papa said to Mama, but she said, "Very well! I'll drive over to the Stones tomorrow and tell Ethan."

"No need for that. I'll tell him. Have to see him anyway about getting the threshing crew lined up. If he's got time to help I suppose we could get some kind of school house built before threshing starts. But if we do, it'll mean you and the girls have to do the chores by yourselves."

"As if we didn't already!" Elsie whispered fiercely.

Mama saw to it that the school was built. Papa would have been willing to let it wait until next year if she hadn't kept after him about it. It was a small building, one room with a vestibule, but it was a beginning, Mama said. Rooms could be added as needed when the men had more time to do it. At least we had a school in time for use this fall. Satisfied with that, Mama gave more attention to the addition and what she would do about her parlor. But not for very long. Papa came back from town one Saturday morning with more young trees for the windbreak.

"Best we get these in right away, Molly. This hot, dry spell is bound to break pretty soon and when it does it could mean rough weather. And later on we'll be busy with threshing."

For the rest of the day all of us worked setting the small trees in dry earth and watering them from the big tank. There had been no rain for weeks, but late that afternoon clouds appeared along the western horizon.

99

"Looks like we might get that rain we've been praying for," Papa said.

I thought he must be wrong. Those clouds were small and far away. Here the sky was clear and the sun still hot. Much as we needed rain, I hoped it wouldn't come right away. If it rained hard before threshing was done, we wouldn't get to go to the circus.

But Papa wasn't wrong about the rain. Those small, far-away clouds kept getting bigger and darker until they were black and covered the whole western sky. The wind died down. The hot, muggy air was suddenly very still. By the time we had set the last tree we were wet with perspiration, glad to get to the house to wash up and change our clothes.

It was after supper that Papa gave Mama the letter from Grandma. Her eyes flashed when she saw that it had been opened. She didn't say anything about that, just read it and began shaking the pages. "Where is the money, Sam?"

Papa didn't look up. "What money?"

"You know what I'm talking about." She began reading from the letter. " 'Your father hasn't been at all well for the past year. We're sending you this money, daughter, hoping you can come now. But if you can't, we want you to use the money to get some real nice furniture for your new parlor . . .' " She stopped, waiting for Papa's answer.

"Oh, *that* money." He wiped his hands on the roller towel. "I figured you couldn't make the trip this year and we can get along without a parlor, so I used the money to buy those new trees."

"But that was my money, Sam. Mother sent it to *me* for a special purpose. Are we so hard up you had to use it without asking me?"

"Well, we're not rich by a long shot! It takes money to build a farm. And anyway, what's yours is mine. So stop talking about your money."

Mama folded the letter slowly and put it back in the envelope. Her fingers were trembling and her face like a thundercloud.

"Sam Bullard, I've taken all I'm going to take! The children and I have worked like mules since we came here. I mean to *have* that trip to Illinois *and* that parlor, and neither you nor all the devils in hell are going to keep me from having them!"

Elsie and Vina and I just stared at Mama. We'd never seen her so angry. And the way she talked! Using those awful words. Papa was staring at her too, open-mouthed, but not saying a word. After a moment he shrugged as if he didn't believe what she had said. "All right, Molly. Just be sure you and the kids keep those trees watered until you go," he said, and got up and went to the kitchen window.

Suddenly the storm inside the house was forgotten.

"Molly!" Papa shouted, "It's a cyclone!"

We rushed to the window. The whole sky was yellow now and a long black thing like a big rope hanging from the sky twisted across the prairie, coming toward our place.

"Close the upstairs windows, girls! Hurry!" Papa yelled. "And bring jackets!" Mama was closing the downstairs windows and doors.

Suddenly a blast of cold wind struck the house. The window shade whirred to the top. Papa grabbed Lucy and Mae and pushed the rest of us out the back door. Outside the wind was so strong we could scarcely stand. Mama held onto all of us while Papa lifted the heavy storm-cellar door. Inside, Mama tried to light the lantern but the wind kept blowing out the matches. Papa stood on the top step, waiting. "Close the door!" Mama yelled above the wind. Papa closed it. The cellar was pitch black. Mama got the lantern lighted in a minute. It's sudden glow gave all of us a feeling of safety. For a while it was very quiet, as if the storm had passed. Then the wind struck again.

It screamed and pounded at the cellar door, pulling it up until the hinges rattled and creaked. We huddled together, holding our breath, and clung to Mama in terrified silence. Suddenly there was a sharp, cracking sound above us. Mama cried, "Oh, Sam, the house!"

Papa put his arm around her and patted her shoulder, but he said nothing. In the lantern light I saw his face. He looked old and frightened.

Suddenly the wind stopped howling, and again it was so quiet we thought the storm was over until the rain hit the earth-covered roof above us. It sounded like a million buckets of water were being emptied all at once. Pretty soon the water began to seep through cracks in the door, getting worse until there was a stream running down the cellar steps.

"We've got to get out of here!" Papa shouted above the noise. "Get up on the benches while I open the door. Maybe we can make it to the house — if there is a house."

It took all his strength to get the door open against the down-pour. He held onto the hand rail with one hand and helped each of us, one at a time, up the stairs. The water was knee-deep in the cellar now. Luckily the house was still there.

"A miracle," Mama said. "Now if I can get the fire going we'll have something hot, and dry out."

We hung our wet jackets behind the door and huddled about the stove, finding it hard to believe that only a few hours ago we were complaining about the heat. Papa went to the kitchen window trying to see what damage the cyclone had done. The rain was still coming down hard so the window was pretty steamy.

"Looks like the barn and windmill are still standing, and the tool shed. I'm surprised the windmill stood up in that gale."

"I'm thankful the house is still standing," Mama said. "You'd better get out of those wet clothes, Sam."

He went to the bedroom. A moment later he yelled, "Molly, come quick!"

We followed her. Papa was at the north window wiping steam from the glass, trying to see out. We crowded around. Lumber was scattered all over the yard!

Papa moaned and cursed. "The whole addition's been smashed to kindling!"

Mama turned away and covered her face with her hands, weeping. "Oh, Sam! My beautiful parlor!"

CHAPTER IX
1892

While wind and hot August sun dried the fields so the threshers could move in, Papa gathered the scattered lumber and piled it in the shed. The path of the cyclone, it seemed, had not been wide enough to damage the stacked grain. Papa said it was still too early to tell how much damage the rain had done.

"When the crops are harvested, what's left of 'em, I'll rebuild the addition, Molly." He blew on his coffee to cool it.

Mama brought a fresh stack of pancakes and put them on his plate. "I've been thinking about that, Sam," she said slowly. "A parlor doesn't seem very important now. I'm so grateful no one was hurt and the house was spared. Why don't we use that lumber to start building a church?"

"Have you lost your senses! All the money I had in the world was tied up in that lumber. I'll be lucky if there's enough of it left to build one room, let alone a church."

"I don't mean for you to contribute the lumber, Sam. We'll sell it to the Church Board. There's enough of it to get the church started."

As usual, when Mama got the best of Papa in an argument, he changed the subject.

"Well, no sense talking about that now. We've got threshing to think about." He pushed back his chair and stood up. "The crew will be here on Monday. The fields should be dry enough by then."

The cyclone and the damage it had done were soon forgotten as once again we bent our back to seemingly endless work. Aunt Hilda, with young Hans cooing in his clothes-basket bed, came to help Mama with the cooking. Harvest was later than usual because of the storm. Elsie and I talked about that. We didn't see how we could possibly finish in time for the circus. But at last the threshing was done and the crew moved on. We awakened to a strange quiet. No longer was there the sound of whirring machines from the fields. The day was bright and balmy. The young trees in the windbreak seemed to dance in the cool morning breeze. Birds chirped noisily. What a wonderful day to see the circus!

Elsie and Vina and I dressed in record time and hurried down to breakfast. Papa was already at the table. "You girls hurry up with breakfast. I want to get an early start on the corn this morning."

"Not today, Sam," Mama reminded him. "You're taking the girls to the circus."

"Circus be hanged! We've got work to do."

"A promise is a promise, Sam Bullard. The girls have kept their part of the bargain, now you must keep yours."

"Don't tell me what I must do! I'm not taking them to the circus and that's final. The corn's late enough as it is. Now eat your breakfast, kids, and get on down to the cornfield. I'll meet you there." He stormed out and slammed the door.

We looked at Mama. Papa just *couldn't* mean what he said! Not after all those months of hard work.

Elsie threw down her knife and fork. "I'll run away! I will, I will!" She pounded the table until the dishes rattled.

Mama had that storm-cloud look. "Calm down, Elsie! Who says you're not going to the circus?"

"Papa did. You heard him," I said.

"Well, for once Papa isn't going to have his way."

"But how *can* we go?" Elsie asked. None of us could believe Mama would defy Papa.

"I don't know how . . . yet. But you're going or I'll make Papa think that cyclone was only a breeze. Now get your chores done."

We didn't wait to ask questions. And never were the morning chores done so fast. Elsie and I milked the cows and turned them into pasture. On the way to the house with brimming buckets of milk, we could see Papa's head bobbing up and down among the tall cornstalks. Vina and Mama were finishing the dishes when we came in.

"Has Papa left for the cornfield?" Mama asked. We nodded. "Then hurry and strain the milk into those crocks and put them in the cellar."

Lucy and Mae were already dressed for town. We changed in a hurry as soon as the milk was taken care of. Mama took a cocoa can from the cupboard and dumped a pile of nickels, dimes and quarters onto the kitchen table.

"I've been saving a little from the egg money," she explained. "It *was* for a Christmas present for Papa, but now . . ."

"Christmas be hanged!" Vina giggled.

Elsie still couldn't believe we were going. "How are we going to get there? Papa took the springwagon to the cornfield."

"Never you mind? We've got better transportation."

Elsie gasped. "Mama! You wouldn't dare! Papa'll skin you alive if you use the surrey."

Elsie was probably right. Last fall when Papa and Uncle Ethan took the grain to the mill in Stebbinsville, Papa had brought back a shiny surrey and a new team of fine grey horses tied to the empty wagon. While all of us stood around admiring them, Papa issued orders. The surrey was not to be used unless he did the driving. So the only time the surrey and new team had been used was when he drove Mama to town, and last Thanksgiving when he drove us to Aunt Hilda's for dinner. He kept the surrey polished and the horses curried and fed and exercised, but they did no farm work. If Mama wanted to go somewhere without Papa she used the springwagon and another team.

Now she was going to take the surrey and greys without Papa's permission!

"Elsie, do you think you and Ann can hitch up the greys without getting your dresses dirty?"

"Sure, Mama. We'll be careful."

"Take them around to the front gate and tie them up. I'll be dressed and have a lunch packed for us by the time you get back."

While we were hitching the team to the surrey I thought how much Mama had changed lately. I'd always thought she was as much afraid of Papa as we girls were. But two or three times in the past few weeks we'd heard her talk back to Papa and make him listen. Now she was going to defy him.

We led the team around to the front gate and tied them. Mama and the lunch basket were ready. Once we were all in the surrey she told Elsie to keep an eye out for Papa until we were well past the house and the cornfield.

The excitement of eluding Papa made us forget for a while *why* we were eluding him. Vina reminded us.

"This team is faster than Papa's, isn't it, Mama? Papa can't catch us, can he?"

"He'll *try* when he finds out we're gone," Elsie said.

"Hush, both of you! Papa promised you could see the circus and you're going to see it. I want you to enjoy it."

"What's going to happen when we get home?" Elsie asked.

"We'll cross that bridge when we get to it."

We had reached the corner where the Millers and the Stones lived across the road from each other. Suddenly I had an idea. "Could we take Aunt Hilda with us, Mama?"

"That's exactly what I have in mind, child. I want to see Uncle Ethan a minute anyway."

Uncle Ethan was working in the yard when Mama stopped the team at their front gate. He put down his hoe and came to greet us.

"We're going to the circus," Vina shouted before Mama could say anything.

"Is that a fact, now?" His eyes twinkled. "I must say you all look mighty pretty in your fancy clothes."

Aunt Hilda came out onto the porch carrying the baby. Mama called to her. "We've come to take you and Hans to the circus with us. Just get your hat. I've fixed enough lunch for all of us."

She came down to the gate. "And Hilda got plenty lunch for baby," she laughed, patting her bosom.

"Please come, Aunt Hilda," Vina pleaded.

"Ja! You bet I come!" She handed the baby up to Mama. "I be joost a minute."

Elsie glanced back anxiously. Vina said, "Stop worrying, Elsie. We may get the whey knocked out of us when we get home, but let's have fun while we can."

I agreed with Vina, but I was worried too. Papa must have missed us by this time. If he caught up with us there would be no circus, and we'd get the licking of our lives.

Mama was talking with Uncle Ethan. "About the lumber Sam saved from the storm. I wouldn't be surprised if the Church Board could make a good cash deal with him for it. But you'd better not say I said so. He's still not convinced we need a church, but maybe you can convince him."

"Good idea. I'll ride over this afternoon and talk to him."

"I wish you would. And if it isn't too much trouble, I'd appreciate it if you were still there when we get back. You see Sam promised the girls they could go to the circus and I mean to see they do. He doesn't know I've taken the surrey and he's likely to be upset when he finds out."

Uncle Ethan laughed. "Between you and Hilda, Sam hasn't a chance!"

With Aunt Hilda and the baby along, all of us relaxed. Even if Papa caught up with us now I doubted he'd risk a tongue-lashing from Aunt Hilda.

As we got closer to town we could see the circus tents. Three of them. They looked as big as a mountain, with a flag flying from the top. Pretty soon we could hear the strange animal cries and a lot of shouting and pounding. We couldn't see anything, though. There was a fence around the fairgrounds where the circus was set up, and the big gate was still locked.

"We're early," Mama explained, looking at the watch pinned to her shirt-waist. "The show won't start until ten o'clock. We'll have time to see some of the sights in town before the parade."

Main street was crowded. I had never seen so many people in one place before, all kinds of people. Some wore long coats and tall hats and carried canes. Most of the farmers were in overalls and wore straw hats. Some boys were barefooted and others were dressed in their Sunday best. Girls in checkered gingham, and others in frilly dresses with big flowery hats, giggled and tried to catch the eye of the older boys. Farm women in calico stood about in little groups, chatting and laughing. Everyone seemed to be having a good time.

"May we get out now, Mama?" I asked eagerly.

"In a minute. I have to find a place to tie up the team."

All the hitching posts seemed to be taken. Mama drove slowly down Main street looking for one not in use. Everyone seemed to be watching us. Was it because of the beautiful surrey and team?

Suddenly from behind us there was a sound like thunder and a blast of trumpets. The band began to play. The greys reared, backing the surrey toward the crowded sidewalk. Elsie screamed. I held onto Mae and Lucy with one hand and clung to Elsie with the other. Vina grabbed me and hung onto her hat. Aunt

107

Hilda wrapped her arms about Hans and yelled something in German. Mama was trying to quiet the team.

"Down, Dolly! Whoa, Lady!" She kept repeating gently. And in a moment they were down — ready to run.

Suddenly a man at the curb seized their bridles and held on, talking to steady them, then led them around the corner to a hitching post.

"They'll be all right now, Madame," he said, tipping his hat. He came around to the side of the surrey to help Mama and Aunt Hilda down. I got a better look at him. He was one of the men I'd noticed earlier wearing a long coat and tall hat. Close-up, he was quite handsome, I thought, except for his black waxed mustache. It made him look like the drummer Elsie had pointed out to me that day on the train.

"Thank you so much for your kindness," Mama said. "I don't know what got into the team. They're usually very gentle."

"That trumpet blast was enough to frighten the Angel Gabriel!" He took a card from his waistcoat pocket and handed it to her. "J. D. Plover, Madame. Attorney at Law, Notary Public and Justice of the Peace. Happy to be of service." He swept off his tall hat and bowed. "May I see you back to Main Street? The parade is about to start."

"We'll be all right now, Mr. Plover. Thank you again."

He tipped his hat and disappeared in the crowd.

Mama gathered us about her. Aunt Hilda, holding the baby close, pushed through the crowd. We followed, and at last were close enough to see.

What a parade it was! Six high-stepping white horses pulled a brightly painted band wagon carrying trumpeters and drummers dressed in blue, gold-braided uniforms. Next came the circus wagons with pictures of animals painted on the outside. Behind the bars wild animals of every kind paced back and forth, making strange sounds. The horses pulling these wagons were covered with white and gold velvet blankets with gold tassels. Even the harness gleamed in the sunlight. Fancy plumes bobbed on top their heads, keeping time to their prancing. Behind the wagons came four elephants, swaying to the music. On the back of each was a lady in pink tights that sparkled and a big hat covered with plumes. *They* must be the ones Papa had told us about.

Elsie dug an elbow into my ribs and whispered loudly, "No wonder Papa didn't want to bring us to the circus! And he's going to be mad as all get out *he* didn't come."

I wasn't going to worry about Papa now. There was too much to see. Several ponies with cute little monkeys on their backs trotted by. Behind them, keeping step to the music, were men and women in all kinds of fancy costumes, and then a big painted wagon with smoke coming out one end and strange music out the other. Mama told us it was steam, not smoke, and that it was a calliope. Last, came the clowns with painted faces and funny costumes.

Then it was over. People began pushing and shoving. Mama and Aunt Hilda kept us together and headed us back to our surrey. "We'd better eat our lunch now and give the crowd time to thin out a little before we start for the fairgrounds."

No one was hungry but we ate anyway, talking between bites and eager to be on our way.

The gate was open when we got to the fairgrounds and there was a long line at the ticket booth. But finally we were inside, following the crowd to the big tent. It was like being inside a mountain. Or inside a beehive. Buzzing voices sounded like a million bees swarming. Elsie and I were too busy looking to talk. Vina kept pestering Mama with questions.

"Why are the swings way up there at the top of the tent?"

"They're not just swings, honey. Those are called trapezes. And if you watch closely you'll see why they are up so high."

"Where are the animals and clowns we saw in the parade? Will we see them again, Mama?"

"Yes. When the show starts. And we'd better find some seats before it does."

Lucy sat close to Aunt Hilda, her eyes big as saucers. Vina was pointing to something at the back of the tent when Mr. Plover took a seat just behind us. He must have followed us! I whispered to Elsie, "Look who's sitting behind us."

Before she could turn, Mr. Plover leaned and touched Mama's shoulder. "Well, hello there! I see you got here all right. No more trouble with the team, I hope."

Mama looked pleased, "Thank you, no. You were kind. The children have never seen a circus before."

Mr. Plover noticed Lucy staring at him. "And how do *you*

like the circus, young lady?" She hid her face against Aunt Hilda shoulder. "Do you like peanuts?" Lucy gave him a timid smile. "Very well, with your mother's permission . . ." He signalled a boy carrying a big box strapped about his neck. "A circus isn't much fun without peanuts." He took four bags from the box and handed one to each of us. We glanced at Mama. She nodded. But before we could thank him there was a loud blast of trumpets and the circus began.

Clowns tumbled into the big circle in front of us, and after them came the whole parade we'd seen on Main street. This time we could see it better. Dressed-up dogs jumping through hoops, ponies and elephants doing tricks, and girls in pretty dresses chased by the clowns. The music was awfully loud, and everything was happening so fast it was hard to see all of it at once. But the long year of hard work was forgotten.

Too soon, it was all over. The animals and performers disappeared behind a big curtain at the far end of the tent. The clowns were the last to go. They were still chasing each other around the ring, doing funny tricks, as the people streamed out, pushing and shoving each other.

"Do we *have* to go home now?" Elsie asked. I knew she was thinking about Papa and the punishment that awaited us.

"Of course we do, child. Now take hold of each other's hands, girls. I don't want you getting lost in this crowd."

"I'm hungry," Lucy wailed.

"After all those peanuts?" Mama scolded.

"Ice cream ve haf', ja?" Aunt Hilda said, pointing to a stand with a red-and-white stripped cover like an umbrella. "Come, *kinder!* Hilda treat."

But when we got to the place there was no ice cream. Just some pink stuff that looked like cotton made into a ball on a stick.

"Goot!" Aunt Hilda exclaimed. "Cotton candy *sehr goot!"* Holding Hans in one arm, she handed a stick to each of us and watched while we tasted it. Then she laughed and asked for two more for Mama and herself.

"Can Hans have some, Aunt Hilda?" Vina asked.

Hilda laughed. "Hans like mama-milk more better!"

We had finished the candy by the time we reached the surrey. Tired, but happier than we had been in a long time, we climbed in and Mama headed for home. The sun was almost down when we stopped at Aunt Hilda's gate.

"I don't see Ethan's wagon," Mama said. "He must still be at our place."

"Is goot!" Aunt Hilda chuckled, and winked.

"I'm not so sure it is," Mama told her. "I doubt Sam is going to understand this was something I had to do."

"Joost cook for him goot supper, Molly, and tonight vear pretty nightgown. Sam vill understand."

I was too tired to wonder what a nightgown had to do with Papa's temper, and too happy to care. Elsie wasn't happy. "Now we'll have to pay for our fun," she warned.

As we neared our gate I saw Uncle Ethan beside his wagon and it was piled high with lumber. Papa was standing with his foot on the hub of a front wheel with a whip in his hand. My heart started to pound. We were in for it for sure!

His back was toward us when we drove in. He didn't turn around, just went on talking with Uncle Ethan who was waving his hands the way he always did when he was excited about something. Elsie climbed out on the side farthest away from Papa and helped Lucy down. Vina got out and I handed Mae to her and climbed down. Elsie went to hold the horses while Mama got out on the other side. Mama's back was toward Papa when she stepped down. I saw him turn and lift the buggy whip but there was no time to call out. The whip came down across Mama's bustle with a sharp crack. The horses reared. Elsie held on until Uncle Ethan grabbed their bridles. Mama jumped clear and turned to face Papa. Her pocketbook fell to the ground spilling its contents.

Uncle Ethan yelled, "Sam Bullard! What's gotten into you?"

"She needed that. Been needing it for a long time!"

Mama said calmly, "He's right, Ethan. That was *all* I needed." She leaned to gather up the things from her pocketbook. Mr. Plover's card was in plain sight. She picked it up and looked at it a moment before she said quietly, "I had a little talk with a lawyer in town today."

Papa glared at her but didn't say a word.

"Striking a wife, I'm told, is grounds for divorce," Mama went on, then turned to Uncle Ethan. "I may need you as a witness, Ethan."

111

"Pleasure to oblige, ma'am," he said solemnly.

Papa dropped the whip and snatched the card from Mama's hand. "What kind of fool do you take me for?"

"I'm beginning to wonder," she said, then spoke to us. "Go change your clothes, girls. Papa will take care of the team and surrey."

"Like fun I will! You took them out. You can danged well put 'em back!" He threw the card at Mama's feet and stalked off toward the fields. She picked it up and put it in her pocketbook, and both she and Uncle Ethan were smiling.

"Did he hurt you, Molly?"

"Goodness, no! Not a bit." Then she laughed outloud. "But I've just found out what a bustle is good for!"

That night we did *not* wait supper for Papa.

He finally unhitched the team, fed and watered them, and put the surrey in the shed. But he stayed out in the barn until we girls went to bed. We heard him come in and demand supper.

"I kept it warm for you on the back of the stove. Help yourself. The bread's in the breadbox."

"Where are *you* going?"

"Upstairs."

"Well, you can give me my supper first. And I want to talk to you."

"The food's there on the stove. We can talk later."

We heard Mama coming up the stairs, and pulled the sheet over our heads pretending to be asleep. She went into Vina's and Lucy's room first.

"Did you say your prayers, baby?"

"Yes, Mama," Lucy said.

"And you, Vina? I see you didn't take time to hang up your clothes."

"I was too tired. But I did say my prayers, honest."

"That's fine. Now go to sleep, both of you. You've had a long day."

Vina was awake now. "Will you really get unmarried from Papa?"

Elsie and I stopped pretending we were asleep. We ran to the doorway.

"Will you, Mama? Will you?" Elsie said. She sounded more hopeful than worried.

"My goodness! Aren't *any* of you asleep? You were all too tired to help me with the dishes." She picked up Vina's dress and hung it in the closet. "What I do about Papa will depend a lot on him."

"But he *did* hit you, Mama. And you said . . ."

"Hush, now! All of you. You have to be up early in the morning even if it is Sunday, remember."

We went back to our bed. Mama blew out the lamp in the other room and went downstairs. As soon as we heard her in the kitchen we hurried to the floor-register to listen. For a while there was nothing but the clatter of dishes in the sink and the creak of Papa's chair.

Finally he said, "I suppose you know I sold Ethan that lumber. You might have to wait quite a while for a parlor."

"I may not be needing a parlor after all."

Silence again for a minute, then Papa spoke in a softer voice. "It takes a man to handle those greys, Molly. You could all have been killed."

"Were you really concerned about that, or . . .?"

"That's a stupid question!"

Mama changed the subject. "How much did you get for the lumber?"

"A lot less than I paid for it, that's sure!"

"Enough to pay back the money Mama sent me?"

His voice rose sharply. "So, you're harping on that again!" The chair creaked. "Didn't that cyclone prove to you how important a windbreak is out here?"

"I know a windbreak is important. Maybe I'm a kind of windbreak too, Sam. For the children *and* you. I want to protect them from growing up without a school or a church or social advantages, and sometimes I have to protect you from your bad temper and broken promises. Today was one of those times."

Again there was a long silence before Papa spoke.

"Molly, if I give you that money what will you do with it?"

"Mama sent it to me for a trip to Illinois. I want to see my folks, Sam. Papa's not well and if I don't go soon I may never see him again alive."

"Come over here and sit down, Molly. Let's talk about this the way we used to." His voice was suddenly gentle. Mama must have done as he asked. "Now then," he went on. "Suppose I give you this money and let you and the girls visit your folks. Will you forget about that divorce nonsense?"

Elsie gasped. "So *that's* why he was being so nice!"

"Shuhhh! They'll hear you!"

Mama said, "It might help, but I can't promise right now, Sam. When I make a promise I mean to keep it."

"So do I, but sometimes there are more important things.

114

Such as a windbreak and getting the crops in on time, and building a church — maybe even a parlor."

"I told you the parlor isn't that important."

"I know you did. That's why when Ethan stopped by today I suggested the Church Board buy the lumber and maybe get the church built before cold weather sets in."

"*He* suggested!" Elsie whispered. "It was Mama's idea and *she* gave up her parlor."

"All right, Molly," Papa went on. "I'll give you the money if you'll let the trip wait until the corn is harvested."

"I guess we can wait that long."

"Then that's settled. Now let's get to bed."

With the prospect of a trip to Grandma's, the corn was gathered and shucked in record time. Mama spent every spare minute making new dresses for us and fixing our old ones. She had written another letter to Grandma, thanking her for the money, but she had said nothing about Papa borrowing it.

Finally it was time. Tomorrow was the day. That night Mama brought the big suitcase from the old soddy and packed it. Aunt Hilda came over to help and promised to see that Papa had proper meals. "Ethan vill help Sam. You 'un *kinder* joost haf' goot visit."

None of us slept much that night. Elsie and Vina and I were up early and did our chores. When we came in with the milk Mama was upstairs. She called to us to come up.

She was sitting on the side of Lucy's bed, her hand on the child's forehead. "She's got a fever, and she's broken out all over. I'm afraid it's the measles."

"Oh, no!" Elsie moaned. "Does that mean we can't go to Grandma's?"

"I'm afraid so. Not right away. If it's the measles you'll probably all catch them. You might just as well unpack the suitcase, girls, and hang up your clothes. I'm sorry. Very sorry."

The doctor came. Lucy had the measles. And before she was over them, Vina got them. Then Elsie and myself. Mama kept Mae downstairs away from the sickroom, hoping she would escape, but she didn't. She was a lot sicker than we had been, it seemed. Or maybe we were so full of disappointment we couldn't feel much pain.

Mama wrote another letter to Grandma.

Papa made no secret about how glad he was we weren't going. And he had his own idea about how we got the measles.

"They never should have gone to that circus. Kids can pick up all kind of diseases in a crowd like that."

By the time we were all over the measles it was too late for the trip. School would start next week.

The new schoolhouse was called *The Goldenrod*, and was about a half mile beyond Aunt Hilda's house, close to where the road branched off toward town. It had one big room with three windows on each side, and an entryway with hooks along one wall for our coats and shelves on the other side for lunch pails. Under the bottom shelf there was room for overshoes. Across the front wall of the schoolroom was a slate blackboard, and in front of that the teacher's desk. Seats with writing desks attached, were placed in rows on each side of the room, with a wide aisle between. Near the front, away from the outside door, was a shiny new pot-bellied stove.

This year we had a new teacher. Her name was Miss Nora Fry and she was young and pretty. From the very first day she made everything interesting and exciting. But we also knew that first day that she would stand for no nonsense from anyone.

"We are very fortunate, pupils, to have this nice new school-house. We must all try to keep it that way. I do not want to find initials or anything else carved on these new desks. Is that clearly understood?"

"Yes, Miss Fry."

At the beginning of each week Miss Fry appointed some of us to various chores. The girls took turns filling the inkwells, emptying wastebaskets, and cleaning the blackboard. The boys carried in buckets of coal when the weather got cold, shoveled snow, and cleaned blackboard erasers. Two of them took turns sweeping out the schoolhouse before they went home. Gus Gruder and Bob Hughes were selected for this task, alternating for a month; after which two more boys would be assigned.

One morning toward the end of the first month, Miss Fry began by reminding us of her warning regarding the school desks.

"I believe you were the janitor last night, Gustave Gruder. Will you come forward, please?"

He got up slowly and walked up the aisle, head down.

"What have you to say for yourself, young man?"

"I'm . . . I'm sorry, ma'am. I guess my knife just slipped."

Everyone giggled. Miss Fry silenced us with a look. "Can you tell me how I can punish your jackknife, Gus?"

"No, ma'am."

"Then I must punish you. Give me the knife, please."

He fumbled in his pocket and pulled out several things along with it.

"Just the knife, please. Now hold out your hand. Even a young man in love has to remember the rules." She put the knife on her desk and picked up her ruler and whacked his hand hard across the palm. Gus squirmed but he didn't make a sound.

"Now you may go to the blackboard and show the other pupils what you carved on your new desk."

"Please, ma'am. Do I have to? I said I'm sorry."

"You weren't ashamed to carve them on your desk where they can't be erased. Do as I ask!"

Gus picked up the chalk and drew a lopsided heart. Very slowly he printed the letters G.G. over A.B. "We know what G.G. stand for. Now you may tell us what A.B. stands for."

He lowered his eyes and shifted from one foot to the other. Then he straightened up and said proudly, "For Alvina Bullard. I think she's the prettiest girl in school and I don't care who knows it!"

Everyone giggled and looked at Vina. She wasn't giggling. Her black eyes were flashing. "Oh, you're just horrid, Gus Gruder!" She covered her face with her hands. I knew then that she liked him a lot, too.

Mama smiled when we told her about it that night. "You'd better not be in such a hurry to laugh at Vina. One of you is likely to be next."

The desks escaped further damage after that but the fence around the schoolhouse didn't. Soon it was well decorated with hearts and initials. Jed Miller carved Elsie's initials with his, and one day I found mine scratched inside one of two entwined hearts. The initials in the other were B.H. I knew Bob Hughes liked me, but I wished it had been Tom Simpson's initials with mine. I thought he was the nicest boy in school.

Goldenrod School soon became the center of the growing community. A couple of weeks before Thanksgiving the School Board decided to hold a box-supper to raise funds for maps and the new books Miss Fry needed. There would also be entertainment provided by the pupils under Miss Fry's direction. We stayed after school to practice our parts in the play we would put on, which of course was about the first Thanksgiving. Those who weren't in the play made drawings of turkeys and pumpkins and pasted them on the blackboard and walls.

This was the first big social event in our Community. Farmers and their families came from miles away. Women and girls brought baskets and boxes of food. Each had tried to outdo the other with fancy decorations as well as good cooking. All boxes and baskets were placed on a long table at the front of the room. No one knew who brought which basket or box.

The room was filled with eager buyers, dressed in their best and buzzing with excitement. Suddenly everyone quieted down. Uncle Ethan stepped up to the table and started the auction. As each box or basket went up for sale there was much whispering and guessing about whose it was. When the sale was made Uncle Ethan announced the name of the owner, and the purchaser joined her. If he had guessed right he was eager to claim his partner. But sometimes I guess he hadn't because he didn't look very happy.

I knew which was Elsie's box and saw her look quickly toward Jed when it went up for bidding. He kept the bidding going and finally got it for two dollars. It was the most any box had brought so far, and Elsie was very proud. I was sure Jed would have paid much more if he'd had to. He made no secret about how he felt toward Elsie.

Uncle Ethan picked up a box shaped like a banjo and covered with ribbons and flowers. "Now here's the basket you've been waiting for, boys! Some couple is going to make mighty pretty music tonight."

A dollar bid came from the back of the room. Joe Nickels stood up. Then Ed Bowers jumped to his feet and bid a dollar and a quarter. The two men kept bidding, raising the price a quarter at a time, until it reached three dollars and seventy five cents. Joe hesitated. He searched his pockets and finally sat down, his face glum.

"Sold to Ed Bowers for three seventy five," Uncle Ethan called. "And the owner of this beautiful box is . . . Miss Nora Fry!"

There was some applause but most people gasped. Everyone knew Joe Nickels had brought Miss Fry to the social, and he probably knew it was her box when he began bidding. He just didn't have as much money as Ed Bowers. He sat still until Ed claimed his companion, then he left the room. We watched him go.

"Mark my word," Papa whispered to Mama. "There's sure to be trouble there before the evening's over."

But the contest between the two boys seemed forgotten as soon as the feasting and fun began. Then it was time for the play. Ed sat with Miss Fry on the front seat where she could prompt us if we forgot our lines. Joe had not come back to see the play. I wondered if he had gone home. I hoped not. I thought Ed was uppity and too sure of himself. I didn't like him even if he was better looking than Joe and had more money.

After the entertainment Miss Fry collected the costumes and put them away. The women helped clear away empty boxes, and stood around in little groups talking in low tones. No one seemed in a hurry to go home. Finally Miss Fry put on her bonnet and Ed held her coat for her. They stepped outside, leaving the door open. Joe was sitting in the buggy, waiting.

"What are *you* waiting around for," Ed asked, loud enough for everyone to hear.

"As if you didn't know! I'm waiting for the lady who came with me."

"Well, wait no longer. Miss Fry is going home with the fellow who bought her basket. That's the rule."

"I brought Miss Fry to the social and I intend to take her home," Joe insisted.

Ed waved his hand toward Joe like he was brushing off a fly. "Drive on young man! Don't be a sore loser."

Miss Fry spoke up. "Shouldn't I have something to say about all this?"

Ed paid no attention to her question. He took her arm and said politely, "Shall we go, Miss Fry?"

Joe dropped the reins and leaped from the buggy. Men and boys hurried out of the schoolroom and formed a ring around

119

the two angry boys. They had their coats off and sleeves rolled up. I tried to squeeze through the crowd to see what was going to happen but Mama pulled me back inside. I could hear Miss Fry trying to stop the fight but no one seemed to pay any attention to her. Pretty soon all I could hear were blows and men cheering.

But when the fight was over Miss Fry was gone.

Uncle Ethan laughed until he shook all over. "Serves 'em both right! Miss Fry left with Elmer Phillips."

I was glad about that. Elmer was Uncle Phil's boy.

One thing I didn't understand was what Papa said when the fight was over. The two boys looked pretty bad but they shook hands like nothing had happened. That was when Papa laughed and said, "Takes a good fist-fight to turn hot-heads into life-long friends, especially if it's over a woman!"

I thought that was a pretty silly way for a boy to try to prove to his girl how much he cared for her. I guess Miss Fry thought so, too. She kept company with Elmer Phillips the rest of that fall and winter. When school was out in the spring she married him.

CHAPTER XI
1892-93

The church for which Mama had given up her parlor did not get built that year. The Board members were all too busy with farm work to think about the promised church, and the lumber they had bought from Papa was not enough for more than a start anyway. Most farmers in the community had suffered some damage from wind and rain. Few could afford to contribute to a church-building fund.

Mama mentioned the church once or twice to Papa, but he insisted he had done his part when he sold the lumber to the Church Board. The rest was up to them. Mama finally decided to take it up with Ben Miller who was Chairman, and let him urge the other members to act. They were Albert Gruder, Seth Jenkins, Hank Rogers and Uncle Ethan. Surely, she said, Uncle Ethan could "light a fire" under them. But apparently he couldn't. All of them came up with good excuses and the promise, "Next year, maybe, when the planting's done."

Papa had several reasons for agreeing with them. First, there was the trip to Grandma's he had promised us. Without us to help with farm work he'd have no time for anything else. And later, when we all came down with measles he used the same excuse. When we were well again the root crops had to be dug and stored for winter, and the butchering done.

Mama did the work expected of her. If she thought about having lost her parlor and being cheated out of the church and the trip to Grandma's *and* the money Papa had "borrowed" and still held onto, she didn't let us know it. But sometimes when she didn't know I was watching her, I thought there was a new kind of firmness underneath her patience. Maybe Papa noticed this too. Ever since their talk that night after the circus he had been careful not to order her around, and he was kinder to us.

One afternoon in early February Papa and Uncle Ethan went to town for supplies, leaving Aunt Hilda and baby Hans at our house. Vina and I looked after Hans so Mama and Aunt Hilda could visit.

121

"If we wait for the men to do it, the church will never get built," Mama said. "We women will have to find some way to raise the money needed."

"How much ve need, Molly?"

"More than you and I can save from our butter-and-egg money," Mama said, smiling.

"Ja. Maybe ve haf' box-social again?"

"Or a pie-supper?" Mama suggested.

"Vas ist?"

"Something like a box-social. We women bake pies and make lots of coffee, and invite everyone to a get-together at the schoolhouse. The men have to buy pie and coffee for wives and children, and a boy buys for the girl of his choice. Afterwards, there are square dances."

"Ja! Ja! *Sehr goot!*" Aunt Hilda agreed, but she wanted to know why the papas would buy pie at a party when they could have all they could eat at home.

"*Because* it's a party," Mama said, laughing.

To make the pie-supper more interesting, they decided to combine it with a Valentine's Day dance. Soon the whole community was buzzing with excitement and plans. Everyone at school was making valentines, and the girls were trying to guess which boy would send her that special valentine.

Papa thought the pie-supper was a good idea although he doubted it would raise much money toward the new church. But he was a good dancer and sang well, and at community gatherings was always in a good humor and let us have a good time, too. All of us were counting the days until the party.

Suddenly, the Wednesday before the party, the weather turned very cold and a heavy snowfall covered the fields. Deep drifts piled up against fences and buildings. We waded though snow to our knees doing the chores, and at night sat around the kitchen table making more valentines. Early Saturday morning, the day of the party, Mama began baking pies. Vina and I peeled apples, and brought several jars of rhubarb and plums from the storm cellar. The kitchen was soon warm and fragrant with good smells of baking.

Papa came in from the barn about noon. "It's starting to

snow again and the wind's getting up. Wouldn't be surprised if we're in for another blizzard."

Mama pushed the curtain aside and peered out. "It does look bad, but those flakes are big; it could let up before nightfall." She put four more pies in the oven. "It better. If it doesn't I don't know what I'll do with all these pies."

"Well, one thing's sure. If *we* can't get to the schoolhouse other folks can't either."

All afternoon we watched wind-blown snow piling up against the side of the barn. Then, toward evening, the wind began to die down. "I think we can make it in the bobsled, Sam," Mama insisted.

Papa agreed that it looked all right now but worried that the wind might come up again and we'd all be caught in a blizzard. "I hate to take that risk. I don't think very many others will."

"They'd better. Unless they want to eat left-over pies for the next two weeks," Mama said cheerfully. "I'm not the only woman who baked pies today."

Papa gave in with no more argument, although I don't think it was because of the threat of eating stale pies; he just didn't want to miss the dance. We had an early supper of hot soup and cornbread, then dressed in warm clothes while papa hitched a team to the bobsled. We piled in, and covered ourselves with warm blankets. As we turned onto the main road the snow had almost stopped.

Mama had been right about the others. No threat of blizzard could keep them from good food and dancing. Even if they did have to buy it a second time! The schoolhouse was filled when we got there with more families arriving every few minutes. Everyone hurried inside, shaking snow from their coats, and gathered around the pot-bellied stove. When the fiddlers' fingers were warm enough the music and dancing began. The storm was quickly forgotten.

An hour or so later everyone had worked up a good appetite. Some of the men started betting on who could eat the most pie, and that gave someone the idea to hold a pie-eating contest. The women encouraged it. The more pie eaten the more money for the church. Each wedge, a fourth of a pie, would cost a quarter. Coffee, or milk, was five cents.

The men lined up alongside the pie table where Mama and Hilda did the cutting and serving. Each bought two wedges and two cups of coffee and carried them to one of the school desks arranged against one wall to be used as tables. Then he crossed to the other side where the women and girls waited to be chosen, bowed before the lady of his choice and escorted her to his table. A special table had been set up for the children, with milk and pie supplied by their papas. A smaller piece of pie cost ten cents.

Jed, of course, chose Elsie. Elmer and Miss Fry paired off. Joe Nickels had brought Nellie Hughes to the dance, and seemed to hold no grudge against Elmer for stealing his "girl". Why should he, I thought? Nellie was very pretty. Mama and Aunt Hilda were too busy selling pie to dance, but later, when everyone was served, Papa and Uncle Ethan bought pie and coffee for them. Gus and Vina were together, no longer shy about each other. And Tom Simpson chose me, which made this a real Valentine party for me.

The pie disappeared as fast as snow before a Chinook wind. Silas Hughes won the pie-eating contest, which wasn't surprising. He was a big man with a "bay-window" large enough to hold half a dozen pies without even feeling full. Afterwards, the women sorted and stacked empty pie-tins and tin cups, and Aunt Hilda counted the money and turned it over to Ben Miller for the church fund.

Mama announced the results of the sale, adding, "I know fifty-eight dollars and twenty five cents won't build our new church, but it's a start. And I hope a big enough sum to prove to our men that we intend to have a church, one way or another." The women applauded, the men laughed. "And now, if the fiddlers aren't too full, I think we should have a few more square dances to shake down the pie we've eaten."

The dancing continued until after ten o'clock. Some of the families had quite a ways to travel. Fortunately the snow had stopped completely, and there was almost no wind now. Everyone had had a good time. All the way home I sang a silent little song. Tom had given me the prettiest valentine I'd ever seen.

With the prospect of a church Mama and Aunt Hilda started planning for it. Both agreed it was a good idea to get the men folk used to attending Sunday morning services instead of pitching horseshoes in the back yard. So it was arranged to hold preliminary services and Bible reading on Sundays in the schoolhouse.

Papa protested strongly. "The kids get enough school during the week. A man needs one day a week to do what *he* wants."

"The children need Bible learning too, Sam."

"Who's going to teach them? Who's going to preach?"

"We'll get a preacher later on when we have a church. I know my Bible pretty well, and so do most of the other women—and some of the men, I might add. We can manage."

Papa seemed to know when there was no use arguing with Mama. The following Sunday he dressed in his best clothes and drove us to the schoolhouse in the surrey. The winds had melted the recent heavy snow. The roads were muddy but passable, the skies clear and the weather warm as spring. While women and children gathered inside for Bible reading, the men remained outside swapping yarns and farm talk. Some times their arguments about politics got pretty loud.

"If you must argue," Mama said on the way home, "why don't you do it right. Form a debating team."

Papa thought it a fine idea. He liked to air his opinions.

When the weather turned cold again the men gathered inside at the back of the room and waited until Bible reading and lessons were over before they got into the usual arguments. But Papa hadn't forgotten about the debating team. As soon as the plowing and planting were done he spent a couple of days driving around to talk to others about it. Enough of them agreed, so the Community Debating Team was formed. The only possible meeting place was the schoolhouse and that was in use on Sunday. They agreed to meet on Wednesdays, once a month.

Not to be outdone, the women headed by Miss Fry, formed a Literary Society. It would also meet in the schoolhouse; the first Friday of every month. If the men wanted to come they were welcome. Most of them came, if only to see what the women were up to. Our schoolhouse had become the busiest place for miles around.

The community had grown considerably since Papa up-

125

rooted us and brought us here. Prosperous farms spread across the prairies and more families were arriving every month. For the young people Sunday School and Literary Society (and the debating team to some extent), provided ways for getting acquainted. After meetings, boys and girls paired off. Some of the girls flirted and giggled so much their parents threatened to leave them at home next time. They continued to flirt and giggle but were careful not to let their parents see them doing it. It all seemed pretty silly to me. Did you have to act that way just because you liked a certain boy and wanted him to like you? I was glad I was still too young and shy for such problems. But Elsie wasn't. She was almost sixteen now, pretty and full of life. She knew Jed Miller was "crazy about her", and liked to tease him. He was only a year older but he seemed older. He was tall and rugged-looking, and his black hair and dark brown eyes made him seem very serious most of the time—and kind of mysterious. All the girls "set their caps" for him but he paid attention only to Elsie. I thought *that* was the way a boy should behave if he really liked a girl.

The Literary Society quickly became very popular in the community. After the program, school seats were pushed back to clear the floor for square dances. Mr. Miller played the fiddle and someone, usually Mr. Hughes, did the "calling". Almost everyone joined in. Even Vina and I sometimes. But I thought watching was more fun. I could tell which boy was crazy about which girl by the way he looked at her when they came together. Aunt Hilda was fun to watch for other reasons. She danced the way she did everything else, with bounce and laughter. Sometimes she bounced so much her thick braids came unwound and then she looked almost as young as Elsie. And when the dance was finished, men and boys scrambled to recover her hairpins. Everyone loved Aunt Hilda because she was always happy. Almost everyone. Some of the women exchanged sly glances when she teased Papa. How could they know this was her way of making Papa like her so she could order him around for Mama's sake? Papa was always in a good mood after Literary Society meetings, and the next morning Mama would be humming to herself as she fixed breakfast. Another reason why all of us enjoyed Literary Society.

What I liked best about them was the reading period. Mama's

wintertime reading hour had whetted my appetite for books, and the Society now opened up a new world of books to me. Grandma had sent Mama a book of poems by John Greenleaf Whittier for Christmas that year. Often she read from it at Literary meetings. Some of the shorter poems were memorized and recited by the older girls. Then one evening Miss Fry announced that the reading of some of the Classics would be added to the regular programs. The audience would select, by vote, the books to be read. For this a list had been prepared. A different member would be assigned to read from the book at each meeting.

The first book selected was *A Tale of Two Cities* by Charles Dickens. Mrs. Hughes was assigned to start the reading. It took most of the winter to finish the long book, but no one minded that; it was very exciting and Mama told us it was a true picture of those times in England and France when life was very hard for everyone. By this time I was deeply in love with books. I day-dreamed about growing up and going to some big city, maybe St. Louis, where there were libraries with hundreds of books anyone who wanted to could read.

For my birthday that fall Mama gave me a beautifully bound book: *Little Women,* by Louisa May Alcott. During the shut-in winter months she read it aloud to all of us. And just before Christmas she read another book by Charles Dickens—*A Christmas Carol.*

The Literary Society was almost two years old when Mr. Evans came to our community. He was a distinguished-looking man, tall and rather thin. Mama told us he had been a professor of English in New York until the doctors sent him west for his health. She said he couldn't be more than thirty and it was too bad he wasn't in good health; but that he soon would be out here where the air was good. He had bought a section of land next to the Hughes place, and I'd heard Papa and Uncle Ethan joking about how little he knew of farming. The important thing, Papa said, was that he was well liked and seemed like a fine man and was probably the best educated man in these parts. Everyone was pleased when Mr. and Mrs. Hughes brought him to one of our meetings.

Most of the men folk came to these meetings to bring their families and to enjoy the entertainment and refreshments; and cared little about the book-reading. They loved the land and their families and most of them worked hard to take care of both. Mr. Evans said he wasn't yet sure he was going to love the land; that he was pretty busy right now trying to understand it! But he admitted he was beginning to feel a lot better. He had no family, so now and then the neighbors stopped by his place to take him a baked ham, a pie or freshly baked bread.

Almost from the first meeting Mr. Evans attended, Miss Fry assigned him to reading the Classics. His voice was deep but it was easy to understand every word although some of them he pronounced differently from the way we had been taught. The book being read at this time was *The House of Seven Gables*. The way he read it was more like he was telling us the story, not reading it. If I closed my eyes I could imagine I was right there in that scary old house.

One evening when he had finished with the chapters assigned no one wanted to break up the meeting and go home. So everyone sat around just talking and visiting. Finally Miss Fry asked Mr. Evans if he would recite something of his own choosing. A dozen voices seconded the suggestion.

He hesitated a moment, then asked, "Would you consider Shakespeare too solemn, ladies? If not I'd like to give you *Hamlet's Soliloquy,* which is one of my favorites and a literary masterpiece, of course."

Miss Fry accepted for the rest of the audience. He waited for the room to quiet, then began dramatically, "To be, or not to be, that is the question . . . . ."

There was scarcely a sound until he had finished, then much applause. I did not understand much of it, and probably several others didn't either, but his voice had held everyone spellbound. I knew that I wanted to know more about Shakespeare, and wondered how old I'd have to be before I could really understand such poems. Later Mama told me Shakespeare was most famous for his plays, and that *Hamlet,* from which Mr. Evans had read, was one of the best known.

Some of the women that first evening were honest enough to admit that they didn't exactly understand William Shakespeare's writings, but they sure did enjoy hearing Mr. Evans recite. Mrs. McCavity went even further. I was standing beside her at the next meeting when she was thanking Mr. Evans for his reading that night.

"Several of us agree that we should make these readings a regular part of our monthly programs. Would you be willing, Mr. Evans?"

"You're most kind. The truth is I have been wondering if I were not taking advantage of your generosity. I mean to say, perhaps I am becoming too fond of the sound of my own voice."

"Nonsense, Mr. Evans!" Mama said, approving the suggestion.

"Would you be willing to consider an alternative?"

"What have you in mind?" Mrs. McCavity wanted to know.

"That you ladies put on some plays of your own. There are many one-act plays which would not be too difficult as a beginning. I've discovered most people have a secret desire, and talent too very often, to act. I worked in many plays in my own college years, and have directed quite a number of them in my classes."

"Wouldn't that be a rather ambitious undertaking?" Mama asked. "Remember, we are farmers' wives with families and little time for learning lines."

"As I have said, we could begin with the simpler plays. Certainly we would not undertake Shakespeare until our players have become somewhat more professional."

Mrs. McCavity interrupted. "I think Mr. Evans' idea is a splendid one, Molly. You know some of us aren't *entirely* amateurs."

Mama smiled. Mrs. McCavity claimed she had studied elocution in St. Louis, and before Mr. Evans joined our Society she had insisted upon reciting at almost every meeting. The members listened but their frequent titters should have told her they were more amused than impressed.

The younger wives in the community who had attended Eastern schools before they married "pioneering" husbands and came to Iowa to build a new life and expand the country, were more modest. They recited when invited to do so and did a much better job. Now they responded with enthusiasm to Mr. Evans' suggestion. "We won't win any prizes," they agreed, "but it will be fun to pretend we're someone else for a while. Farm work isn't exactly romantic!"

Nevertheless, they also agreed, farm work had to come first. They could "pretend" only in the early spring and late summer when farm work was less demanding. Of course, not everyone had a chance to participate in the actual plays, but now holiday programs were more varied so no one was slighted. Mr. Evans sent to New York for several copies of one-act plays he felt were suitable. Somehow the players found time to learn their parts. Theater Night soon became the Society's biggest event.

It was during one of the productions in early March the following year, that the telegram came.

Uncle Ethan had gone to town that afternoon but had promised Aunt Hilda he would be back in plenty of time for the play. It was half over when he tiptoed down the aisle and sat down next to Mama. Papa was waiting in the entryway with Mae and Hans who had become restless. Uncle Ethan handed a yellow envelope to Mama. I knew that meant a telegram and telegrams usually brought bad news.

Mama tore it open and tears filled her eyes when she showed it to Aunt Hilda. She whispered to Elsie sitting next to her, and all of us left as quietly as possible.

"Is the show over?" Papa asked.

Mama handed the telegram to him. "Read it to the girls, Sam." Papa read slowly:

Your father passed away yesterday Stop Funeral next Sunday Stop Come if you possibly can.

It seemed a long way home that night. We rode in silence.
Only the sounds of horses' hooves and the crunching of carriage wheels on the hard-packed road broke the awful stillness.
Now and then a frog croaked, a cricket chirped. I looked up
at the full moon riding high among billowy clouds and thought
about Grandpa. I couldn't believe we would never see him
again, yet I knew Grandpa was somewhere up there beyond
the white clouds with God.

"If only you had let me go last spring, Sam!" Mama sobbed.

"You could have gone. I told you you could."

"But without the children. Now none of us will ever see
him again." She was crying softly. Elsie and Vina began to
cry too. I choked back tears. Somehow it didn't seem right to
cry when I knew Grandpa was with God.

"Don't take it so hard, Molly," Papa said gently. "You still
have Mother Dauber, and I'll see to it you and the girls get to
Illinois for the funeral."

"How *can* we go? I know you spent the money mother sent."

"I had to spend it. But I've got friends. They'll loan me a
little until after harvest. So stop crying, please. It won't bring
your father back." He turned in at our gate and helped Mama
down.

The house seemed unusually quiet as if it knew the sorrow
we felt. Even the air seemed to be standing still. The box-elders
cast long shadows in the moonlight. An owl in the cottonwood gave a mournful cry.

Papa put the team and surrey away by himself. We followed
Mama into the house and went upstairs to change our clothes.
It was past our usual bedtime but there was much to be done
to get ready for the trip. Mama would be up most of the night.
Papa didn't take off his coat when he came in. "I'm going to
ride over to see Ethan. I think he'll be able to loan me some
money. Might as well find out tonight." He started out, then

turned. "Couldn't you leave one of the older girls here to look after the house and meals? I'll try to get Jed Miller to help with the farm work."

"Oh, Sam! How *can* I leave one of them? It wouldn't be fair. Elsie and Ann are the only ones old enough to be of any help."

"I'll stay, Mama," Elsie volunteered.

This wasn't like Elsie. Usually she made more fuss than any of us about "going some place". Or *was* she being unselfish? Maybe Jed Miller had something to do with it.

"Are you sure you don't mind, dear?" Mama asked.

"Someone has to stay and I'm the oldest."

Mama hugged her. "That's my big girl! I'll write out instructions for you before I go to bed. The batch of bread I'm baking should last until we get back. And there's plenty of sausage left, and salt pork for the beans. You can use one of the hams in the smoke-house if you want to." For a while she seemed to forget her grief in her concern for the living.

We had a very early breakfast the next morning. Elsie said her goodbyes. Papa drove us to the station and put us on the train. He kissed all of us goodbye and held onto Mama quite a while as if he thought she might not come back.

It was very sad not to see Grandpa at the depot in Roanoke. A stranger met us and drove us to Grandma's house. She hugged Mama and both of them cried a while, then Grandma came to each of us and kissed us. The house was as beautiful as I remembered it, but now it was very still and the shades were drawn. Grandma took our wraps and hung them up, then led us into the parlor. A black coffin with silver handles stood on two chairs. She drew back the cloth that covered it. Mama looked in and began to cry very hard. We cried too until Grandma took us into the kitchen.

"You children must be starved after that long trip." She talked like we'd just come for a visit. Maybe she too thought it wasn't right to cry when she knew Grandpa was with God.

We ate the soup and cornbread she set before us. Mama drank a cup of coffee but she wouldn't eat anything. We slept that night but I don't think Mama did. Her eyes were red and swollen the next morning.

The funeral would be held Sunday afternoon. Grandma's

neighbors came, filing into the parlor solemnly for a last look at Grandpa. All of them were crying when they came out. Finally four men went in and carried the coffin out to the waiting hearse. Vina and I rode with Mama and Grandma in a neighbor's surrey. Lucy and Mae stayed with another neighbor.

I had never been to a funeral before. Part of the time, on the way to the church, I wished I had been allowed to stay with Lucy and Mac at Grandma's house. At thirteen, even though Mama often said I was "old for my age", death and weeping filled me with fear and strange questions. Why must everyone wear black? And why did folks cry so much if Heaven was a beautiful place?

Listening to the minister that day, and the weeping, I decided Grandpa's friends were crying because he was a good man and they missed him so much. And then I knew how much we were going to miss him forever and ever, and I began to cry.

Gradually Grandma's house again became the way we remembered it. The shades were let up. Bright spring sunshine poured in. The lilac bushes outside the bedroom windows where Vina and I slept were beginning to bloom. I thought their fragrance the most wonderful perfume in the world. Green showed on the lawn and the big cottonwoods that shaded the house were bursting with fat buds and tiny green leaves. During the day we helped Grandma in the garden and at night, after supper we sat in the beautiful parlor where she kept her treasures—the stereoscope and slides, and the red plush album.

Much of the time Mama and Grandma left us to ourselves. They seemed to have a good deal to talk about. I wondered if Mama would tell Grandma about Papa keeping the money she had sent her, and about his hitting her with the buggy whip. And about Mr. Plover.

We had been at Grandma's two whole days now. Right after supper that night she brought a long thick envelope from the desk in Grandpa's study and put it on the table beside Mama's plate.

"Your father left this for you, Molly. He asked me to take good care of it and to be sure you got it, not Sam."

Mama opened the envelope and her eyes got as big as eggs. Then she began to cry. "Is all this for me?" she sobbed.

"Yes, dear. Your father didn't hold much with making a

will. He left me the house and money in the bank. I knew he planned to leave something to you but I didn't know how much until now. There should be a note in the envelope."

Mama removed the contents of the envelope and it was our turn to get big-eyed. It was the biggest stack of paper money any of us girls had ever seen. She found the note Grandpa had left but she was crying too much to read it. Grandma took it and read it aloud. "This is for you, dear daughter, to use as you wish. I suggest some kind of investment, however. I would not want Sam to squander it on some wild scheme. Your husband is a good man, Molly, and a hard worker, but not a very good manager I'm afraid. Take care of yourself and the children. God guide you in making a good life for all of you."

Mama cried for a while before she picked up the money and put it back into the envelope. She did not tell us how much there was, but I knew it was a lot because the stack was big and the note on top was for a hundred dollars.

"But what will I do with it? I can't carry this much money on the train."

"Don't worry about that now. We'll think of something before you have to leave." She went to the kitchen and brought Mama a cup of hot coffee. "Now I guess we'd better get these dishes cleared away."

Our visit with Grandma was almost over. She and Mama talked while they packed. We were going home tomorrow. When the knock sounded on the front door, Grandma went to answer it. And came back with Uncle Phil.

He went to Mama and took both her hands. "I'm so sorry, about your father, Molly. He was one of the finest men I ever knew. The world won't be the same without him."

Tears came to Mama's eyes. "Thank you, Phil. I only wish I could have come before he left us, but you know what farm work is like."

"I do, indeed. But you're looking well. How is Sam, and Elmer and Nora?"

"They're all fine. Elmer's doing very well with his farm."

At last Uncle Phil noticed the rest of us. "My goodness! How you've all grown! Come here, Lucy, and give old Uncle Phil a big hug." Lucy was in his arms with a leap. He held her while he went on talking to Vina and me. "Iowa seems to be treating you both well. I'll swear I've never seen two prettier young ladies."

Vina blushed, and I guess I did too, because Uncle Phil said, "You're going to have to get used to compliments. And from boys a lot younger than I am."

We thanked him. "We're so glad you came to see us before we left," I said.

He turned to Mama. "My goodness! They really are grown up, aren't they." A moment later he added, "I don't want to seem disrespectful at a time like this, Molly, but I was hoping you and your mother and the girls could pay a visit to the old farm before you go back."

Grandma made the decision for all of us. "I don't think I should, not so soon. But I think it would be good for Molly and the girls. Why don't you go, Molly? Leave Mae here with me."

"Well, I would like to see the old farm. But it doesn't seem quite proper."

"Oh, fiddlesticks! You've earned a vacation. Your father would want you to take it. And I'd say you'll be well chaperoned with three grown-up children along, if *that* is what's worrying you."

"Please say yes, Mama," Vina and I pleaded.

"Well, if Grandma thinks it's all right we'll go tomorrow."

"Fine! Fine." Uncle Phil said. "I have to get back now, but I'll meet the first train to Saunemin in the morning. Don't disappoint me, please. It gets there pretty early so you'll have the whole day."

The train got to Saunemin about nine o'clock the next morning. Uncle Phil was waiting as he'd promised. When we got to the farm Vina and I ran ahead to open the gate. Everything looked almost the same as before, except that the house had been painted. White with yellow trim. The catalpa trees Mama loved were still there close to the house. The lilac bushes were beginning to bloom. Our swing still hung from a limb of the big cottonwood in the back yard.

Vina and I left Lucy to enjoy the swing while we explored the haymow and the creek that ran through the pasture. Everything seemed just the way it was when I used to take the cows to pasture. Iowa seemed a long way off.

Lunch was ready when we came back to the house. We'd

gathered as many early-blooming wild flowers as we could find. Mama took them and put them in a vase and set it on the table. It was covered with oilcloth instead of a tablecloth. The windows looked bare without Mama's frilly curtains.

Uncle Phil must have guessed my thoughts. "We took the curtains down when Fred and I moved in. A couple of old bachelors didn't need 'em. Besides, who would keep 'em washed and ironed?"

Mama smiled. "What did you do with your house, Phil?"

"The two Mott boys live there now. They help out with the farm work. It gets a little too much for Fred and me at planting and harvesting."

"Where is Fred? Will he be in for lunch?"

"Not likely. He went to Minonk this morning. But he's sure to be back before you leave. He's grown into quite a man. Taller than I am, now."

After lunch Uncle Phil and Mama sat on the porch and talked. When we asked, she said it would be all right for us to go to the creek, but to be back in time for an early supper, we had a train to catch. We spent the whole afternoon by the creek. Fred still hadn't returned when we got back.

"I don't understand what's keeping him," Uncle Phil said.

"I'm sorry we won't see him, but I don't think we should wait any longer. Be sure to give him my regards, won't you." She turned to me. "Are you girls ready?"

Uncle Phil drove us to the depot. We were tired but happy. Lucy slept and Vina and I talked about the fun we'd had and how mad Elsie was going to be when she found out we'd been to the old farm.

"Do you think Mama will tell Papa we went?" Vina whispered.

"I don't know." But I wondered about it. Mama was looking out the window paying no attention to us. Was she trying to decide about that? Or about what to do with the money Grandpa had left her?

Some of the answers I learned when I heard Mama and Grandma talking the next morning. They were in the kitchen when I came downstairs. Vina and Lucy were still asleep.

"That trip to the farm sure did you a lot of good, Molly. You look as fresh as a daisy."

136

"I'm glad we went, but I don't think Sam is going to be pleased that we did. Sometimes I think he's a mite jealous of Phil, though he has no cause."

"Well, you don't have to tell *him* that," Grandma said. "It's good for a man to be jealous sometimes. Makes him appreciate you more."

"Father didn't have to be jealous to appreciate you."

"Your father was a very rare man, Molly. It's not going to be easy for me to do without him."

Neither spoke for a while. I stayed in the dining-room, not really meaning to eavesdrop but I couldn't help hearing when Mama said, "I had a talk with Phil about the money father left me and I've decided what to do with it, but I'll need your help. Phil will . . . . ."

At that moment Vina and Lucy came clattering down the stairs and I didn't hear the rest of it. Mama and Grandma were now talking about something else.

"When faith goes, everything goes," Mama was saying. "There have been times out there in Iowa when I felt mine was as burned up as the grasslands in August. I don't want that to happen to my children. They must have a church and a proper home to grow up in, and Sam has to stop expecting them to work like farm hands."

All of us would agree with that!

We left the next morning. Grandma went to the train with us and promised she would try to pay us a visit next year if we couldn't get back to Illinois. She stood on the platform waving goodbye as the train pulled out. I thought she looked awfully lonely, and wondered when we would see her again.

Mama seemed very thoughtful all the way back to Iowa. Several times when I said something to her she didn't seem to hear me. I wanted to ask her what she was going to do with the money Grandpa left, but I didn't think she would tell me. Besides, if I asked she'd know I'd overheard part of the conversation and I was ashamed to have her know that. Maybe she'd tell Elsie and me when we got home.

CHAPTER XIII
1893

Papa wasn't at the station to meet us when we got home. "He probably didn't get my letter," Mama said.

I was remembering the first time we arrived in Stebbinsville. Papa hadn't met us then. A stranger had driven us home, and I thought of that awful first night in the soddy. Now at least it was spring and we knew our neighbors. Someone from our community was sure to be in town.

"We'd better go over to Harris' Feed Store and see if we can get a ride out," Mama decided. "I just don't understand Papa not being here. He should have had my letter by this time."

Mama carried Mae. Vina and I took the suitcase and Lucy tagged along behind us. The feed store was at the end of Main street, two blocks from the station. We walked slowly changing hands with the heavy suitcase. Delicious smells of fresh bread and cinnamon rolls came from the open window of Saunders' Bakery. A little farther on was Jacob's Harness Shop. The door was open and tangy smells of leather and oil and tobacco smoke drifted out from the shop. When we came to Miss Millie's Hat Shop we set the suitcase down and exclaimed over the many bonnets in the window.

We had scarcely reached the feed store before Uncle Ethan came out with a bag of cotton-seed meal over his shoulder. "Well, bless my soul! When did you get in, Molly?"

"A few minutes ago. Sam was supposed to meet us. I guess he didn't get my letter in time."

"You can ride out with me, soon as I pick up the mail." He smiled. "Seems I recall another time Sam didn't meet you and I took you and the kids home."

"And I'm thinking Sam doesn't much care whether we come home or not."

"Don't blame him too much. We've all been mighty busy this spring. Hardly had time to get to town for supplies."

When he came back from the postoffice he handed Mama

138

our mail. "Looks like we're going to surprise him," she said. "My letter to him is still here."

As it turned out, we were the ones to be surprised.

Uncle Ethan let us out at the back gate and went on home. "Come over soon as you can, Molly. Hilda'll be mighty glad you're back," he said as he drove off.

Mama took the suitcase and started toward the house. Suddenly she set it down and shouted. "Sam! What on earth . . . .!"

Papa was standing in the kitchen door with a shotgun in his hands.

Lucy screamed. Mama ran toward the house. Vina dropped Mae's hand and ran after her. I just stood there, too scared to move. Was Papa going to shoot all of us? But why? We hadn't done anything wrong.

Mama grabbed his arm, and he lowered the gun. "I'll get that low-down pup! And when I do . . . ."

"What on earth are you talking about? Where's Elsie?"

"She's gone. Gone, I tell you!"

"Where, Sam? What happened here?"

"I don't know where they went, but I'll find them and when I do that Jed Miller will wish . . . ."

"Stop talking in riddles! What has Jed to do with all this?"

"Everything, the sneaking pup! I hire him to work for me and he runs off with Elsie behind my back the first chance he gets."

Mama got him into the kitchen and calmed him down. I brought the suitcase and set it down in the kitchen. Vina took Lucy and Mae upstairs. When I started to follow, Mama said, "Will you fix us some coffee, Ann. I think Papa needs some, and I certainly do."

One thing was soon clear. Elsie and Jed had eloped. I didn't know why but I was sure Papa had had something to do with it. Elsie was only sixteen and she wouldn't run off with Jed Miller or anyone else without a good reason. Papa must have given her a good reason. I remembered the times she had threatened to run away when Papa had done something terrible to her. Now she had done it.

"You'd better go change your dress, dear," Mama said when the coffee pot was on. "Papa and I have some talking to do. I'll bring the suitcase up later."

139

If she knew we could hear through the floor register she'd probably forgotten about it in her concern for Elsie. Vina and I listened. And after a good deal of prodding Papa told Mama what had happened.

Elsie and Jed had been doing the morning milking while Papa pitched down fresh hay. They were making a game of it, trying to see who got the bucket filled first, laughing as they tried to outdo each other. Papa had told them to cut out the foolishness and tend to milking. He said they hadn't paid any attention to him. Pretty soon Elsie had jumped up shouting she was the winner, and in her excitement upset the bucket of milk. Papa slapped her for not listening and for wasting the milk. He told her to get the other bucket of milk to the house before they spilled it too, and told Jed to get the stalls cleaned out and no more horse-play. Then he went to the fields with a load of manure. When he came back Jed and Elsie were gone. So were Elsie's clothes.

All was quiet for a while after Papa finished his story. Then Mama said a strange thing. "Well, Sam Bullard, you've got the son you always wanted."

"Jed Miller? That sneak-thief is no son of mine and never will be! When I catch up with him he'll wish he'd never been born!"

"Shouts and threats won't change anything. Whatever Elsie has done you're responsible for it, Sam Bullard. The way you've bullied the children for years, I'm surprised they haven't all run away. You'd better be thankful it was only one of them, and that Jed Miller is a very fine young man."

"Oh, he is, is he? What would you say if I told you he got her to sneak out to the hickory grove with him night after night when they were supposed to be in their beds?"

"I'd say that if a girl hasn't a proper place to entertain her young men friends, she has no choice but to resort to some other place," Mama said quietly. "We should have had a parlor long before this, and I mean to see we have one before Ann and Vina and Lucy elope with some boy maybe not as fine as Jed."

"Last summer you said a parlor wasn't important. *You* told me to sell the lumber to the Church Board."

"A church is important too. There's no reason why we

shouldn't have both. And we *are* going to have them. If not here, then back in Illinois. The old farm looks mighty nice. Phil has taken good care of things."

"Do you mean to tell me you went out to see Phil with your father not even cold in his grave? What kind of a woman are you, Molly?"

"A pretty blind one up to now, I'm afraid. And you can set your mind at ease. I didn't go to the old farm to see Phil. He came to Roanoke to see us and invited the children and me *and* mama to come out before we returned here. Mama didn't go, of course, but the children and I did. Surely you didn't think we'd go to Illinois and not visit the old farm?"

"Well, a visit is all it's ever going to be. I'm not taking you back there."

"I didn't ask *you* to. I can go without your help."

"Oh, you can, can you? Seems to me you're acting mighty independent all of a sudden. Not that you haven't always been stubborn at times. But you've got something up your sleeve. What is it?"

"Not up my sleeve, Sam. In the bank. Papa left me enough to provide a parlor *and* a trip back to iIllinois if that becomes necessary."

The long silence below told us Papa hadn't thought of that possibility. When he spoke again his tone was quite changed. "Well, now! That was pretty nice of the old gentleman. How much did he leave us?"

"He left nothing to *us*. He left it to me."

"All right, to you. But how much?"

"As I said, enough to build and furnish a parlor *or* move a woman and four daughters to Illinois if necessary."

"All right! You don't have to tell me if you don't want to. Soon as the spring work is out of the way I'll rebuild the addition so you can have your parlor. Right now it seems to me we ought to be worrying about Elsie, not parlors. You're sure taking *that* mighty calmly."

"No sense taking it any other way. We'll hear from Elsie when she knows we're back."

"Well, *I'm* not waiting to hear from her! I'm going over to Miller's tomorrow to find out if he knows where that good-for-nothing son of his has taken our daughter."

141

"I don't think you'll find out anything. Eloping children seldom tell their parents where they're going."

"You don't have to get sarcastic about it. This is serious. Don't you realize that girl's only sixteen?"

Mama laughed lightly. "Who should know better? Maybe it is time you started realizing that she *is* sixteen, not a child."

Papa pushed his chair back from the table with a scraping sound. "Well, I've got to do the milking. It's good to have you home, Molly. I've missed you." We heard the screen door close. It was safe to go downstairs. Mama was humming softly to herself as she started supper.

"Will Elsie ever come back, Mama?" I asked.

"Of course she will, honey. I wish she'd waited for a proper wedding, but Jed's a fine boy and wherever they are he'll take good care of her and bring her back soon to see us. Elsie loves all of us. Just remember that."

"Not Papa. She always hated him. Now I think I hate him too. Even more than I used to hate him."

Mama put down the pan she was washing and put her arms around Vina and me. "Hate is a terrible thing, darlings. It hurts you more than the person you hate. Don't ever forget that. I know Papa does things he shouldn't a lot of times, but that's no reason for you girls to hate him. I don't think Elsie hates him either even if he lost his temper sometimes and whipped her too hard. He expects too much of you girls, I guess, because he's angry with himself. I know you don't understand that now, but you will when you're older. Everything is going to be all right. You'll see."

She picked up the suitcase and carried it upstairs and told me to unpack. Vina was setting the table when I came downstairs again. Supper smelled good.

Papa was whistling when he came in. "By golly, it's good to have you home, Molly!" he said as he set the pails in the drainboard and kissed her. "I haven't had a decent meal since you left."

He washed up at the sink and sat down. Elsie wasn't mentioned again. And all during supper he laughed and joked and asked questions about the old farm.

On Sunday, everyone expressed sympathy to Mama over the loss of her father, but no one said a thing about Elsie. After

Sunday school the older kids gathered in little groups and I knew they were talking about Elsie and Jed. When they saw me coming they stopped talking.

But on Friday at Literary Society meeting, the women spoke openly to Mama about the elopement. Jed Miller, they said, was a fine young man and would make Elsie a good husband. Sure she was pretty young, they agreed, but sometimes that made for a very happy marriage, they said.

"I hear Mr. Miller is going to buy that quarter-section next to the Rogers' farm and give it to the young couple for a wedding present," Mrs. Hughes reported.

"Yes," Mama told her. "Mr. Miller came over to tell us about it right after I got back from Illinois."

I hadn't seen Mr. Miller at our place since we got home, but he must have talked to Mama. She wouldn't say that if he hadn't.

"It will be nice having the children nearby," Mrs. Gruder said. "Elise's pretty young to manage her own home without *some* help." Mama agreed with that.

The men joshed Papa about his new son-in-law. All of them said he couldn't have a finer one than Jed. Papa seemed to have forgotten his threats the night we came home. Now he talked like Elsie's marriage to Jed was *his* idea.

On Monday spring housecleaning began. It was already late, and with Elsie gone the sooner we got at it the better. Mama surprised us by making some changes too. She wasn't going to wait for the new addition to be rebuilt before she had her parlor. She moved Vina and Lucy into the bedroom I'd shared with Elsie. The furniture from the downstairs bedroom was brought upstairs and set up in the other bedroom. Our sleeping arrangements would be crowded, but Mama said it wouldn't be this way for very long. Meantime the downstairs bedroom would make a suitable parlor, and the sitting-room could also be used as a dining-room.

Papa wasn't at all pleased about the change, but he didn't get angry as we expected he would. All he said was, "Seems to me you could have waited until we built on another room or two."

"We've waited too long for a parlor as it is," Mama said.

"I'd like you to drive me to town tomorrow to get furniture for it."

Papa looked surprised. "I *presume* you intend to pay for this furniture you're talking about. I sure can't, not the way things are right now."

Mama didn't say anything. Papa went on, "Your father must have left you a good deal of money the way you're spending it."

Mama smiled. "Enough for parlor furniture anyway."

The "temporary parlor", as Mama called it, seemed to us girls a magnificent one. How could she want anything more beautiful than this? The new rug was not a homemade one. It made the floor look like a whole field of moss roses. New ecru curtains at the windows were soft as sunlit clouds. The sofa and matching chair were covered with green plush. A quarter-sawed dark oak table with a fringed velvet cover stood in the center of the room. On it was a big lamp with a round base and shade made of white glass decorated with red roses like the carpet.

Whatever objections Papa had to the parlor were soon forgotten when he saw the big leather reclining chair Mama had purchased for him. He carried it in and set it down near the new base-burner, and stood there admiring it for a minute or two. Then he grabbed Mama and kissed her several times.

"Oh, Sam, stop acting silly!" Mama pushed him away and fussed with her hair. But she was smiling.

For the next several weeks Papa was a changed man. He didn't grumble that Elsie was no longer around to help with the outside work, and he was kinder to all of us. I thought of what Mama had said about not hating him. If he'd stay the way he'd been lately it wouldn't be hard not to hate him. We might even get brave enough to say we loved him.

The last week in April the rains came. Day after day water poured from the sky as if a dam in the clouds had broken. It washed out a lot of the oats crop before the roots were deep enough to hold.

Papa came in from doing the chores, drenched to the skin. "I'll swear, Molly, I don't know why *any* man in his right mind wants to farm! If it isn't one thing it's another! Too

144

much rain, or so gol-darned dry everything burns up. If this keeps up much longer we'll have nothing left."

Mama brought him a cup of coffee. "Get out of those wet clothes and drink this, you'll feel better. The rain can't last much longer."

But it did. For the rest of the week it came down steadily. School was closed, and none of us went outside unless it was absolutely necessary. Papa did the milking, fed and watered the stock, and worried about the crops. Finally, on Saturday, the sun came out. As if in a hurry to dry things up, it was unseasonably hot. Papa saddled one of the horses and went to inspect the damage.

"It's pretty bad," he reported. "I'll have to replant the oats as soon as the ground's dry enough. If it stays as hot as it is today I can start the first of the week. I'd better get supplies from town today while I have time."

But when he returned from town that evening it wasn't his damaged crops he talked about.

The moment he sat down to supper he said, "Lucky I went to town today, Molly. Danged lucky! I ran into Jim Edwards who owns one of the hardware stores on Main street. He's a good-hearted old cus but not much of a business man. Seems he extended credit to a lot of farmers last fall, and now with all this rain, looks like he's going to lose his shirt."

"That's too bad. But why is that lucky for you?"

"It's our opportunity, Molly!"

"I don't see . . . ."

"It's like this. Jake Spaulding has invited me to go into partnership with him and take the hardware store off Jim's hands. We'll split fifty-fifty. Jake will manage the store until I get the crops harvested."

"Who is putting up the money for this? Jake?"

"No, I'm to do that. You see, Molly, I thought we would invest what your Pa left you. No sense just leaving it lay there in the bank."

"That money is already invested, Sam."

Papa's mouth fell open. "The devil it is! What . . . . ."

"I didn't tell you how much father left me because he said you would want to invest it in some hair-brained scheme. And it seems he was right. Now I'm going to tell you how much and what I did with it. Father left me five thousand dollars and I bought back the farm at Saunemin."

Papa jumped to his feet almost upsetting the table. "Well of all the stupid fool things to do! If you wanted to buy a farm why didn't you ask my advice, buy land here in Iowa where we can look after it? Oh, no! You had to let Phil sell you a bill of goods. You're a silly, sentimental fool!"

"Yes, I'm sentimental about that farm, Sam," Mama said calmly. "But Phil sold me no 'bill of goods' as you put it. I bought the farm for exactly what he paid for it, and it's a much better farm now. I'd say that makes it a good investment."

Papa sat down again. "The hardware store would have been a whale of a lot better investment. But if my own wife hasn't the sense to see that I'll just have to get the money some other way. I *am* going to buy that hardware store! With or without your help!" He banged his fist so hard on the table the spoons in the spoonholder rattled. Then he gulped the cup of coffee Mama had set before him earlier, and stalked out the back door leaving his supper untouched.

He also left us to wonder what he meant about getting the money some other way. Could he force Mama to give him the money? Make her sell the farm in Saunemin? It was still almost too good to believe that she had really bought it. But I now understood what she and Grandma had been talking about in the kitchen that morning. Mama had left enough money with Grandma to pay Uncle Phil when he delivered the deed, and put the rest in the bank in Roanoke where Papa couldn't get at it or find out how much she had. But now Papa knew how much Grandpa had left her. What was he going to do? Mama didn't seem worried.

A few days later I began to have a horrible feeling that I knew what he was going to do. Whenever I was with Papa out of Mama's hearing he asked me a lot of questions. Did we kids really go with Mama to Uncle Phil's? Were Mama and Uncle Phil alone in the house? Why didn't one of us tell him about the money Grandpa left? The questions sounded like he meant to make trouble for Mama and Uncle Phil, and I didn't know what to do.

The next morning Papa hitched the greys to the surrey and went to town. He'd scarcely spoken to Mama since he learned what she had done with her inheritance. He ate in silence and did the work about the farm mostly by himself. Watching him when he wasn't asking me questions, I knew he was planning something. Now I guess he was going to do whatever it was.

Papa came back about noon. With him was a well-dressed man. Papa called to Mama from the buggy. "Set another place, Molly! We've got company."

When the stranger got out of the buggy we saw he wasn't a stranger at all. He was our friend, Mr. Plover. Suddenly I was afraid. Was Papa going to divorce Mama? Was that how he was going to force her to give him the money for the hardware store?

Mama went out onto the back stoop. Mr. Plover tipped his derby hat to her. "So *you're* Mrs. Bullard! I'm pleased, indeed, to see you again."

Papa looked from one to the other. "By golly, you *weren't* joshing were you?"

"No, I certainly wasn't." She turned to Mr. Plover.

"Please come in. If you don't mind a simple meal we're happy to have you join us." She picked up her skirts and led the way into the kitchen.

"What a charming place!" Mr. Plover exclaimed, glancing about.

Mama thanked him. "Sam, why don't you and Mr. Plover wait in the parlor. I'll have lunch ready in a few minutes."

Vina and Lucy came in. Mama told them to get cleaned up. Mr. Plover was lunching with us. "What's he doing here, Mama?" Vina asked.

"He is our guest. Now go wash up and comb your hair."

All through lunch Papa was gay and well-mannered. He usually was when we had company. "Have another piece of meat, Plover. And some of Molly's plum butter. When it comes to cooking, Molly's the best in the county."

"Thank you, no more meat. I'm saving room for that delicious-looking apple pie. Or are you saving that for dinner, Mrs. Bullard?"

Mama smiled. "There will be plenty for both meals." She cut and served and poured the coffee.

Papa finished a big piece and two cups of coffee. "Now

you children go on outside and play. Mama and Mr. Plover and I have business to discuss."

Play! If we hadn't had company he'd have found work for us to do.

Vina and Lucy went outside. I went into the sitting-room and left the door open a crack so I could see and hear. I *had* to know what Papa was up to.

Mr. Plover took some papers from his pocket and put them on the table. "Mrs. Bullard," he began, very businesslike, "I represent the newly formed firm of Spaulding and Bullard, hardware merchants. All the papers for the partnership are here, signed by both parties and filed. However, on this one paper I must have your signature. It is a mortgage on your husband's farm for a thousand dollars."

Mama took the paper and looked at it for a minute or two. "I don't approve of mortgaging the farm for a business venture Mr. Bullard knows nothing about," she said firmly. "He is a good farmer. I think he has enough financial responsibility right here."

"There is some risk in everything, Mrs. Bullard," Mr. Plover argued. "In farming the risk is perhaps greater than in most businesses; risks over which you have no control. Wind, rain, hail or drought can wipe out all the work and profit very quickly. It seems to me Mr. Bullard is wise in attempting to provide another source of income as a bulwark against such an eventuality. His lack of experience in the hardware business I consider a minor problem. Mr. Spaulding, an experienced merchant, will manage the business. Your husband will be more or less a silent partner, taking care of his farm as you very properly suggest, and collecting half the profits from his investment."

Mama smiled. "I can't imagine Mr. Bullard being a silent part in anything."

Mr. Plover laughed politely. Papa, for once, *was* silent.

For half an hour I squatted near the door listening to the arguments. Mr. Plover met Mama's objections, one after another, with convincing reassurance. At last Mama said, "Very well, Sam. I'll sign the mortgage but I think you're making a big mistake."

It wasn't long before Papa learned she was right. He could

not be a silent partner. Soon after the mortgage papers were signed, he insisted the firm name be changed to Bullard and Spaulding. "It sounds better, and I put up the money," he told Mama. Apparently the thousand dollar investment was more important to Mr. Spaulding than whose name came first on the new sign they put up.

Gradually Papa began to spend more and more time in town. There were things, he said, that required his attention. "And I have to keep an eye on my investment, don't I? And *two* eyes on Spaulding. He's too liberal with credit. But he raises merry-Ned when *I* want to order more supplies. Says we have to watch our inventory. But how the devil can we sell what we haven't got?"

Mama didn't argue. She told him she had said all she had to say before the mortgage papers were signed. Most of the farm work was now left to us with some help from our neighbors when they had the time.

Elsie and Jed had come back, as Mama predicted, a couple of weeks after we returned from Roanoke. Now they were settled on Jed's new farm, and Elsie had her own house to look after. She avoided Papa, but she drove over to see us whenever she was sure he wouldn't be around. One good thing about Papa spending more time in town was that we saw Elsie more often. She seemed so grown-up, older than sixteen. But I could tell she was happy because she now laughed a lot, and she hadn't before getting married.

One afternoon, a couple of months after Papa had gone into the hardware business, Mama had a visit from Mr. Spaulding.

"If you have any influence over your husband, Mrs. Bullard," he said emphatically, "for heaven's sake keep him at home! He's driving more customers away from the store than a quarantine sign. Most farmers have to have some credit until harvest. A few of them I admit are poor risks. But Sam can't say no without insulting the poor devils. It's hard enough for most of 'em as it is. I've talked myself blue in the face trying to make Sam see you can't treat customers like a herd of cattle. It's done no good. I thought maybe you could reason with him."

"I appreciate your coming to see me, Mr. Spaulding," Mama

said quietly, "I'll do what I can, but I'm afraid Mr. Bullard isn't the kind of man anyone can reason with, least of all me."

After we had gone upstairs that night Mama mentioned the matter to Papa. He exploded. I went to the floor-register to listen.

"Why, that no-good snivler! Trying to blame me, is he? Well, it won't work. He's supposed to be the business manager. Some manager! I got a look at the books today. No wonder we aren't making any money. He's giving credit to every Tom, Dick and Harry in the county. *Our* business is all figures in a ledger. The cash customers take their trade to Acme Hardware. One cyclone or hail storm and where are we?"

"I'm afraid you and Mr. Spaulding will have to work it out between yourselves, Sam. The children and I have enough to do to keep the farm going. And I wasn't in favor of your buying the store in the first place, remember?"

The arguments between Papa and Mr. Spaulding must have continued. Listening to Papa's report to Mama I concluded Mr. Spaulding believed in buying only what he was sure could be sold quickly. Papa, on the other hand, was a plunger. He wanted to "stock up", and signed contracts for merchandise which bound both partners to payment whether it was ever sold or not.

"If *we* haven't got what a customer wants," Papa argued. "he can danged well get it at Acme. We need that cash business."

Mama listened to his reports but kept out of the arguments. Things went on this way until the first week in November. The weather was cold. Papa was content to stay at the farm and let Mr. Spaulding run the store. "It's too cold for much business anyway," he said.

One afternoon Uncle Ethan stopped by our place on his way back from town. "What's happened to the hardware store, Sam?" he asked over a cup of coffee.

"Nothing's happened to it. With this bad weather business is slow."

"They tell me in town the store hasn't been open for several days."

"Spaulding's probably sick. I'll drive in tomorrow and find

out. Thanks for letting me know, Ethan. I've got quite a bit tied up in that store."

The next day was Saturday. Mama and I went to town with him. She had promised me a new dress for my birthday, and I was to pick out the material.

We found the hardware store closed and locked. Papa unlocked the door and we stepped inside. It was very cold here too. The floor had been swept clean and the merchandise was neatly displayed in cases and on counters. It looked a lot better than when I'd been in the store before Papa bought it. He went to the office at the back of the store and opened the door.

"What in thunder?" he yelled.

We hurried to see.

The safe door stood wide open.

It took only a moment to discover that the cash-box was empty. The ledgers were stacked on the desk, and on top of the pile, weighted down with a piece of lead pipe, was a letter from Mr. Spaulding. Papa read it aloud.

> Dear Sam—I hate to do this to a partner but there just ain't no room in this business for two managers. I have taken the cash and left you the inventory. You ordered most of it against my advice. I hope you can sell it and break even, maybe. I tried hard to make a go of the store but you wouldn't let me run it right. So I guess before you make any more enemies for us I better clear out. The business is all yours.
>
> Respectfully
> Isaiah Spaulding

Papa was so mad it was a while before he got his breath. Then he exploded. "Why, that dirty low-down scoundrel! I'll have the law on him for this! *Nobody* can do this to Sam Bullard!"

Finally he calmed down enough to examine the books. Mr. Spaulding not only had taken the cash from the safe but had drawn out all the money in the bank. Six hundred dollars all together. Papa was spitting mad now. He slammed the books into the safe and shut the door. "Come on, Molly! We're going to see Plover."

Mr. Plover listened to Papa's story. "I'm sorry about all

151

this, Sam, but I'm afraid there isn't a thing you can do about it. Under the law, each partner is liable for the total liabilities of the firm. Whether you like it or not the business is yours. And the debts."

"But that . . . that scoundrel *stole* my money!"

"In a sense, that's true. If you can find him you can take him to court and force a somewhat more orthodox dissolution of the partnership. But that would be a costly procedure— and you'd still be liable, along with Spaulding, for the firm's debts. It would seem wiser to take your loss, Sam, and spend the same money to reopen the store."

Papa just sat there saying nothing, his head bowed. His mouth trembled like he was going to cry.

Mr. Plover tried to reassure him. "Don't take it so hard, Sam. It isn't as bad as it might be. Your creditors can't take what you haven't got. Our laws see to that. But surely you can persuade the creditors to give you time to reorganize and collect from *your* creditors."

Papa didn't seem to hear him. Mama went to him and put her hand on his shoulder. He looked up and I saw there were tears in his eyes. "I'd counted on the store to make enough money to rebuild the addition, Molly. I just can't believe the money's all gone. And our farm too."

"Maybe we can find a way to save both, Sam. Come on, dear. Let's go home."

My birthday present was forgotten.

CHAPTER XIV
1893

The trip back to the farm was solemn and silent. Papa held the reins but he sat motionless, his shoulders slumped, staring into the distance. The team knew the way home. Mama sat stiffly erect, her coat collar turned up to protect her face from the cold. I sat between them, comfortable and warm under the laprobe. But I felt a lot older than the fourteen I would be on my birthday next week. I knew there would be another change in our lives. Papa had decided the other changes, but I knew Mama would decide this time. And maybe this time it would be better.

I remembered all the times I had wanted to go back to Saunemin, even prayed God to let us go. Now, when it seemed we might have to go back, I wasn't sure I wanted to. There were too many things we would have to leave behind. Our friends, school, the Literary Society, Aunt Hilda and Uncle Ethan and Hans, and our nice new house and Mama's fine new parlor. And Elsie and Jed. Oh, we couldn't leave *them!* And they couldn't leave their new farm.

Now, for all our sakes, I prayed God to let us stay in Iowa.

As we neared the house Papa stirred and spoke for the first time during the trip. "It's a good farm. Molly. We ought to get a good price for it. More than enough to pay off the the mortgage and make a new start somewhere else."

"Somewhere else?" Mama's tone was sharp. "We are *not* leaving Iowa, Sam."

"What else can we do? A man knows when he's licked. If we don't sell the farm the bank will, and the creditors will take the hardware store."

"We'll cross that bridge when we get to it. Right now I'm too cold to think about it, and you have the chores to do."

Papa said no more. Mama climbed down and helped me out. Papa drove on to the barn. Lucy and Mae met us at the kitchen door. "Did you bring us candy, Mama? Did you?"

That too had been forgotten along with my birthday present. She took off her coat and hung it up, then sat down and put an arm around each of them. "I'm sorry, babies. Papa had some unexpected business in town today, so I forgot the candy I promised you. But next time I go to town I'll bring you two kinds. Now run along and get ready for supper before Papa comes in."

Vina sensed something was wrong. "What happened, Mama?"

"Nothing that can't be remedied, dear. We'll talk about it later. Ann, change your dress, then you and Vina go help Papa with the chores. I'll have supper ready by the time you're finished."

Vina pestered me all the way to the barn. "What happened?" I told her as much as I had time to tell before Papa came out of the surrey shed.

"You kids go ahead with the milking. I have to change my clothes."

As soon as we were alone Vina asked, "Will we really move back to Saunemin?"

"Not if Mama has anything to say about it, and she will have this time."

"But I thought she *wanted* to go back there. Wasn't that why she bought back the farm from Uncle Phil?"

I couldn't answer that.

We ate supper that night in tense silence. Vina and I were bursting with questions but we didn't ask them. Finally Papa leaned back in his chair and looked straight at Mama. "I've made up my mind, Molly. We're going to do what you've always wanted to do. We're moving back to Saunemin."

There was a long silence. "Let's not be hasty, Sam. We don't have to decide about that tonight."

"I've already decided. You're going to get your way."

"How do you know it *is* my way now? Things change, Sam."

Papa sputtered. "You mean to tell me, after all these years of begging me to move back to Illinois, now you've changed your mind?" He shook his head in disgust. "By thunder, *nothing* changes like a woman!"

"Many things have changed. Elsie is married. She and Jed have their own farm here now. We have a fine farm, a nice house and school, and good neighbors. The girls have their friends. It's true I didn't want to come here and for a long

154

time I wanted to go back to Saunemin. But we have a good new life here now, Sam. God has given us a great deal to be thankful for."

Papa jumped up as if Mama had slapped him. "*God* hasn't given us anything! *I* worked for everything we have here. These buildings, the windbreak, fences. *I* built 'em, God didn't!" He pranced about the room like a skittish horse. "The Lord giveth and the Lord taketh away, eh? Well, let me tell you, Molly Bullard, all the *Lord* has done is take away! The giving I've done."

We were terrified. No one spoke. Mae began to cry. Mama picked her up. "I'm going to put her to bed. And the rest of you better go to bed too. I'll take care of the dishes."

We knew she wanted to talk to Papa alone, so we quickly cleared the table and went upstairs. As soon as Lucy was in bed, Vina and I wrapped ourselves in a blanket and huddled over the register. Pretty soon Papa took up where he left off.

"If you think I'm going to stand by and let the bank take everything I've worked for, you don't know Sam Bullard!"

"What do you propose to do about it?"

"Sell the danged place and move back to Illinois. Or go farther west and get a new start. We made it here. We can make it somewhere else."

"Always a new start, Sam. How long do you think the girls and I can stand that kind of life? Or you? You're not getting any younger."

"So now I'm an old man, eh?"

"You will be if you keep on making new starts the rest of your life. And I'll be an old and broken woman. Is that what you want, Sam?"

"Stop talking nonsense! We've got the farm in Saunemin. Now you don't want that. What *do* you want?"

"Right now I want to finish these dishes and go to bed. We're both too tired to decide anything tonight."

If Papa answered we didn't hear him. The kitchen was quiet except for the sounds of dishes being put into the cupboard. After a while there was a creak of Papa's chair and the thump of his heavy footsteps on the stairs. Vina and I scrambled into bed. The door across the hall opened and closed. A few minutes later Mama came upstairs and opened our door. Satisfied we were all asleep she closed it softly.

Sunday was bright and clear but cold. Mama hummed a hymn as she fixed breakfast. I set the table while Vina dressed Mae. Lucy sat on the edge of the woodbox impatiently waiting for Papa to come in from the barn so we could eat. Lucy was always hungry. The amount of food she could put away at one meal was enormous. She was getting as round as a butterball.

Papa came in with two brimming pails of milk and set them on the kitchen cabinet for Mama to strain and put away. He was glum and silent through breakfast. As soon as he finished he put on his coat and started out.

"We'll be ready to leave in an hour, Sam. Aren't you going to change your clothes?"

"What for?"

"For Sunday school and church. Have you forgotten it's Sunday?"

"I'm not going. You take the kids if you want to go. I'll hitch the team to the surrey."

"Very well. But I think you should go too."

"And let everyone pound me with questions about the store? Not on your life!"

"I doubt that would happen. And some Bible reading might be good for you," she said, and I knew she meant the way Papa had talked last night.

"Just the same, I'm not going." He went out banging the door.

With the nice weather, everybody it seemed had turned out for Sunday services. The schoolhouse was filled. Uncle Ethan and Aunt Hilda, with Hans on her lap, were sitting near the door. They had saved seats for us, one too many without Papa.

"Where's Sam?" Uncle Ethan asked when we were seated.

"He decided not to come today," Mama said, and smiled. "You see he's not exactly on speaking terms with God this morning."

Uncle Ethan grinned. "I see."

Little Hans began to squirm. Aunt Hilda let him down and held onto his hand. The Bible reading was about to start. She looked awfully fat, but I knew that was because she was going to have a baby. Elsie had told me all about it and a lot of other things, the last time she visited us and we had a chance to talk alone. I was glad it was Aunt Hilda who was having a baby, not Mama. Aunt Hilda had time to be sick, Mama didn't. She had too many problems to solve.

After the services, Uncle Ethan walked with us to our surrey. "You girls go on. I want to talk to your mama."

We went. They walked slowly and I couldn't think of any excuses to stay close enough to hear what they were saying. Whatever it was must have been good. Mama hummed all the way home. And whenever Mama hummed softly to herself she was planning something.

Monday was washday. Mama had the boiler on the back of the stove and the tub set up on a bench in the kitchen when we left for school. Papa, still silent and moody, had gone to the barn as soon as he finished breakfast. I wondered how long he'd go on like this. All of us, except Mama, were waiting for him to do some dreadful thing. But the week passed and nothing happened.

On Saturday, at breakfast, Mama asked, "Are you going to town today, Sam?"

"No."

"Then I'll go. We need groceries."

"You can all go if you want to. But not in the surrey. I'll hitch up the springwagon for you."

"Very well. The children will enjoy it. They haven't been to town for quite a while, and the weather is warmer today."

We washed the dishes and swept the kitchen and made our beds. And all of us were dressed and ready when Papa brought the springwagon to the back gate. It was a beautiful winter day, warmer than usual this time of year. Everyone was in a gay mood once we got away from Papa's gloom. All the way to town we sang, or played richman-poorman-beggarman-thief with the fenceposts along the road.

When we got to town Mama gave me the grocery list. "You and Vina can get the groceries. I have some business to take care of." She took Lucy and Mae with her and started off. "Oh, yes. You can spend ten cents for candy if you want to." She smiled. "And Ann, you can pick out the material for your new dress. I'll meet you at Nelson's in about an hour." She hadn't forgotten my birthday!

It was almost noon when she came into the store. We'd taken the groceries to the springwagon and I'd spent the last fifteen or twenty minutes trying to decide which material I liked best. Mama liked the soft brown worsted, but she let me have the green challie that I liked, even if it was more expensive.

"A girl has only *one* fourteenth birthday, honey. She should have something she wants. Now let's see about a pattern, shall we?"

When we left the store I was too happy to wonder where Mama had been all morning. She hadn't said a word about getting my new dress when we left for town. She'd saved it for a surprise! And now she had another surprise. She steered us down the street to Olson's Restaurant. Eating in a restaurant was a rare treat, and expensive. I wondered if she had forgotten to bring sandwiches. Or had she planned it this way to make our day in town more interesting?

All the way home Mama was exceptionally cheerful. I knew it must be because of the "business" she had attended to but she didn't say what it was. I dreaded to reach home. Papa would be waiting for us, gloomy and silent. Mama would stop smiling and we girls would speak in whispers and walk on tip-toe. Papa was sitting at the kitchen table adding up a column of figures when we came in. He glanced up and grunted, "Well, it's about time you got back."

Mama didn't let it bother her. "Will you take care of the team, Sam? I'll change and have supper ready in a jiffy. Ann and Vina will help you as soon as they've changed."

Papa gathered up his papers and put them away, then took his coat and went out.

Supper that night was a feast. Pork chops and fried potatoes, baking powder biscuits with plum butter, and apple pie. Everything Papa liked best. I thought of Aunt Hilda's advice the day we came back for the circus. "Cook for him goot supper . . . ." Mama had certainly done that tonight. It ought to put Papa in a better mood. It didn't.

As soon as the supper table was cleared Papa brought writing paper and pen and ink from the sitting room. "You go on to bed, Molly. I've got to write to Phil, let him know we'll want our farm back come March first."

"Whose farm?" Mama teased.

"*Our* farm! What's yours is mine. Can't you get that through your head?"

"You don't have to write Phil tonight. A lot of things can happen between now and March first. Why don't you come to bed now. We've all had a long day."

"No sense putting it off. You go on to bed if you want to." Papa's letter to Uncle Phil, sealed and stamped was on the kitchen table the next morning. Again he refused to go to Bible Reading, but he handed the letter to Mama. "Ask Ethan to mail this for me when he goes to town tomorrow. He usually goes on Monday."

Mama put the letter in her pocketbook. After services, when Uncle Ethan walked with us to the surrey, I waited for Mama to give him the letter. She didn't. I saw it in her pocketbook when she opened it on the way home to get a handkerchief.

For a while Papa was less gloomy. I knew the letter had something to do with his better mood. What would he do if he knew Mama had not given it to Uncle Ethan? I didn't know why she hadn't but she must have had a good reason.

Two weeks passed. Papa's temper sharpened. The mortgage on the farm would come due March first, he said. "No sense waiting 'til they *put* us out. I want you to be ready to move before that happens."

"It's quite a while before March first, Sam. Providence has a way of helping when we need it."

"Providence, my eye! It won't pay the mortgage."

Mama went on with her work. She didn't start packing.

A few days before Thanksgiving when Papa came back to town he was in a temper. "Why in thunder doesn't Phil answer my letter? He'd had plenty of time. He can't be *that* busy this time of year. Maybe he thinks I don't mean what I said."

"Would that surprise you?" Mama asked. "After all the bragging you did about Iowa — rich virgin soil and no trees to plow around, and room for a man to stretch and grow. It *doesn't* make sense, Sam, that you'd suddenly want to turn your back on all of it and go back to Illinois."

"A man does what he has to." He got up and went outside.

The weather turned cold again. Sharp winds whipped the

snow into flurries of white dust along the roads. Driving was difficult. Mama did not go to town on Saturday and she did not ask Papa to go. "We can get along with what we have. If we need anything by Monday I'll ask Ethan to get it for us."

It was getting dark when Uncle Ethan stopped by Monday evening to leave the supplies he'd brought us. Papa was at Ben Miller's place helping with butchering. Uncle Ethan carried the groceries into the kitchen, then took a packet of mail from his pocket. "You didn't ask me to pick this up for you but I did anyway."

Mama thanked him. As soon as he had left she looked through the mail. One letter she tore open quickly, her face tense. Then she smiled as she read. "Well, girls, we won't be moving to Illinois no matter what Papa says. And tomorrow, Ann, you and I are going to town regardless of the weather." She folded the letter and put it in her apron pocket.

"But school, Mama . . . . ?"

"You're all going to have to miss one day of school. Papa will be helping Ben again tomorrow, so Vina will have to stay at home with Lucy and Mae. We won't say anything to Papa about the trip to town until we get back."

On the way to town the next morning Mama talked to me like a grownup. The wind had died down but it was still cold in the open surrey even with the heavy laprobe and side curtains.

"You are the oldest at home now, Ann. You're big enough to know what I've done and why I've done it without telling Papa." She slapped the reins and we bounced along over the frozen ground. "Your father is a fine man, Ann, and he's the best farmer in the whole county. His temper is his worst enemy. Sometimes he lets it get the better of his judgment and then he loses his 'pioneer' courage. As you get older you'll understand that women in this new country have to do a lot more than cook and wash and raise children. We have to be strong enough to do all those things, but we also have to help our menfolk keep their pioneering spirit. Because if they lose that there will be little or no progress in this country. Somehow God gives them the strength to want to pioneer, and He gives women the strength to do their work and keep the men from becoming discouraged."

We rode a while in silence. Then she looked at me and smiled. "Now I want to tell you about the problem we faced when the hardware store failed, and what I have done about solving it."

Upon Uncle Ethan's advice—because Papa was too hurt and worried to think straight—she had gone to see Mr. Close that Saturday when she had taken all of us to town with her. She had asked Mr. Close to find a buyer for the farm in Saunemin. The letter that came yesterday, she said, informed her that he had found a buyer and the money was now waiting for her at his office.

"It will be more than enough to pay off the mortgage when it is due. We can also pay the hardware bills and reopen the store."

"Oh, Mama, I'm so glad. I didn't want to go back to Saunemin. I don't think you did either. But Papa is going to be very angry because you didn't tell *him* about all this before."

"For a while, maybe. But he'll get over it." She glanced at me and smiled. "As soon as he gets his 'pioneering spirit' back."

Mr. Close was sitting at a big roll-top desk, his back to the door, when we entered his office. He was a small dark man with thinning black hair. He swung around at the sound of the door opening and a big smile lighted his face. He hurried toward us, hand extended.

"*Good* morning, Mrs. Bullard! And a fine morning it is, indeed! We were mighty lucky to find such a good buyer for your property this time of year. Yes, ma'am, mighty lucky!" He shook hands with Mama and drew up two chairs near the pot-bellied stove. "Sit right down and warm yourselves. It's right nippy out today."

"Thank you, Mr. Close. This is my daughter, Ann."

"Ah, and a mighty pretty lass she is, too. How are you, young lady?" He took my hand and pumped it with too much vigor. I wasn't sure I liked him even if he had kept us from having to move back to Saunemin.

We sat a while, warming our hands and feet. Suddenly Mr. Close's breezy manner changed to sober business. He took a paper from his desk and handed it to Mama. It was a deed with a check attached.

"That's a good deal of money, Mrs. Bullard. I've been giving some thought to the best way for you to use it—best for your purposes, that is. May I tell you about my conclusions?"

"Please do. I shall appreciate your advice."

"Very well. With that money you can meet the mortgage on your farm and pay off what is owed by the hardware store and reopen it. *Or,* and this would be my advice, you can invest all or most of it in income-producing property. Once you have title to this new property you can easily mortgage it for enough to meet your present obligations. Income from the property will permit you to pay off the new mortgage when it is due. This way, Mrs. Bullard, you would have your principal, or its equivalent, intact. The hardware store, once its obligations are paid, can easily become a profitable business. So can the farm."

I was surprised Mama seemed to understand all he was saying.

"What you suggest, Mr. Close, sounds reasonable. But I'd like to think about it, talk it over with Mr. Plover and my husband."

"Of course! Of course! And if you do decide to invest this money, I have a couple of good buys I'd like to show you. Solid, well-constructed buildings right here in Stebbinsville where you can keep an eye on them, with good steady rental income."

Mama stood up. "Thank you very much. I shall come back to see you after I've talked to Mr. Plover. If he approves I'm sure my husband will. And of course I'd want Mr. Plover to see the buildings you have in mind."

"Fine. Fine, Mrs. Bullard. I'm here to serve you, and it's a real pleasure."

I was glad to get outside. The room had been too hot and listening to Mr. Close, trying to understand what he was saying, had tired me. "He sure has a lot of energy, doesn't he, Mama?"

She smiled. "He certainly does, child. But he knows his business, too."

Mr. Plover's office was a couple of blocks down the street. It would be nice to see him again. I knew he liked Mama, and felt sure any advice he gave her would be right. His office was a lot nicer than Mr. Close's. There was a carpet on the floor, and big red leather chairs at each side of a table with magazines on it. Bookcases, with glass doors, filled with leather-bound books lined one wall. Mr. Plover sat behind a large carved desk in a leather chair that turned when he did. He got up and greeted us like old friends.

"Delighted to see you both. What brings you to town so early in the day. Not more trouble with the hardware store, I hope."

"In a way, yes," Mama said. She sat down next to his desk. I took one of the chairs by the table and looked at the magazines. "Indirectly, I should say. You see I've sold our farm in Illinois, with Mr. Close's help. Payment has now been made and Mr. Close has advised certain investments as the best way to use the money. I'd like your advice."

"I'll be happy to help of course. Can you give me the details?"

Mama related exactly what Mr. Close had said. She *had* understood it!

"It sounds feasible, Mrs. Bullard. A great deal depends upon the properties he has in mind. What they may be worth both in terms of purchase and mortgage potential. And of course the stability of the present tenants. Do you know where the buildings are?"

"Here in Stebbinsville," he said. "But I don't know which ones. He'll be glad to show them to us I know."

"Very well. We'll have a look at them, then stop by the bank and have a talk with Amos Booth. His opinion on the transaction will be most valuable."

I think Mr. Close was surprised to see us back so soon, and Mr. Plover with us. "You've made a wise decision, Mrs. Bullard," he said seriously.

Mr. Plover smiled. "Mrs. Bullard hasn't bought the building yet, Joe. She merely wants to see them."

"Naturally. Wouldn't have it any other way. Sit down a minute. I'll be right with you." He checked the fire in the stove, then shrugged into his coat and took a derby hat from a clothes-tree. We went out ahead of him. He hung a sign on the door indicating when he would return.

Walking down Main street Mr. Close remarked, "I suppose you know most of the buildings along here are owned by the

163

Stebbins family. Practically all the older buildings and a good many of the new ones. The buildings I'm going to show you are a part of that estate. Old Josiah Stebbins' estate, that is. If they weren't they wouldn't be for sale at any price the way the town's growing. But Josiah's gone now and Mrs. Stebbins is old. Their sons have gone East to make new fortunes. They have no use for property out here.''

He stopped in front of Bruckner's Grocery Store. "This is one of the newer buildings, Mrs. Bullard.''

"But I thought Mr. Bruckner owned the building?"

"No. He's been renting it for five or six years now from the Stebbins' Estate. Ever since Frank built it and then decided to go East and join his brothers. Come on in and let me show you around.''

It was one of the nicest buildings on Main Street. We'd been buying groceries there for almost four years, but I guess Mama hadn't paid much attention to the inside before. While she and Mr. Close and Mr. Plover wandered about and talked with Mr. Bruckner, I looked around trying to imagine how it would feel to *own* a grocery store. Of course we'd only own the building, but would that mean we'd get our groceries for less money?

The other building Mr. Close showed us was also one of the newer buildings and one we'd been in many times. Miss Millie's Hat Shop occupied the street floor. Upstairs was Bertha and Erma Whitely's Dress Salon. They were old maids, Elsie said. But everyone liked them, and they did make the prettiest dresses!

We didn't go inside today. Just looked the building over, then went back to Mr. Plover's office without Mr. Close. "I'll let you know what Mrs. Bullard decides, Joe.''

For more than an hour Mama and Mr. Plover talked. I looked at magazines but couldn't help hearing some of their conversation.

"I've tried to study it from all angles, Mrs. Bullard, and I honestly believe you couldn't invest your money more wisely. You'll have a good monthly income from the buildings. The tenants are as reliable as any in town. And the value of the buildings will hold up for several years since they're fairly new and well constructed, and the town is growing rapidly.''

"Very well. Let's see how Amos Booth feels about them as a mortgage risk. I hear he's a very careful man — where the bank's money is concerned."

Mr. Plover smiled. "He certainly is. Which will make your investment all the more sound if he approves." He got up and helped Mama with her coat. "When we finish at the bank, may I have the pleasure of taking you and your pretty daughter to lunch?"

"You're very kind. I'm sure we would both enjoy that, wouldn't we, Ann?"

"What, Mama?" I had to pretend I hadn't heard.

"Mr. Plover has invited us to lunch when we finish our business at the bank."

I waited in the bank lobby while Mama and Mr. Plover went into the president's office. Amos Booth, President, was lettered on the door. Everything must have gone the way they wanted. They were smiling when they came out.

Lunching with Mr. Plover was a lot of fun. He talked about so many interesting things and he made Mama laugh with his witty remarks. I hadn't seen her so happy for a long time. Some of it probably was due to Mr. Plover's company, but most of it I felt sure was because the day had gone well for her in business matters. As nearly as I could understand all of it, it looked like we would still have our farm here, and the hardware store, as well as owning two buildings in town. That is, we would have all this as soon as Mr. Plover and Mr. Close drew up all the papers for her to sign. But what if Papa had to sign them too? Suppose he refused? I didn't want to think about that.

When we came out of the restaurant I walked a little behind them so they could finish their talk.

"I hope you know how much I appreciate all your help today," Mama was saying. "Mr. Bullard is still too upset over Mr. Spaulding's behavior to be entirely rational in such matters as these. I'm sure he will approve of what I have done when I can explain it to him."

"I've no doubt about that. Still, it is not easy for a man to accept such business talents from a woman. You're quite remarkable, Mrs. Bullard."

I agreed with that. I didn't agree that Papa would approve of what she had done today.

CHAPTER XV
1893

The wind seemed colder on the way home. Dark clouds were piling up on the western horizon.

"Looks like we're in for more snow before Thanksgiving," Mama remarked, urging the team to a faster pace.

After we had left Mr. Plover, we had gone back to Bruckner's to get the things we needed for Thanksgiving dinner. "We've a very great deal to be thankful for this year. More than ever before in many ways. I do wish Grandma could be here with us."

"Why can't she be? There's still time for her to get here."

"Yes, there's time. But she doesn't like to travel in this kind of weather. It's hard on her at her age. Old people feel the cold more than we do, you know."

The sun dropped behind the cloud bank as we turned in at our back gate. Papa didn't seem to be around. I hoped he was still at Ben Miller's. I think Mama hoped so too. The first question she asked Vina when we entered the kitchen was, "Has Papa come back?"

Vina said he hadn't. "Then you go help Ann with the team and surrey. I'll start supper. Papa will be here soon and he'll be hungry as a bear. Though how anyone can be hungry after butchering all day is something I never could understand."

Vina and I had most of the chores done when Papa got home. I thought he would be pleased about that but he didn't say anything. Just went on into the barn to feed the stock.

All during supper we waited for Mama to mention the trip to town but she didn't. Most of the conversation was about plans for Thanksgiving dinner. This year Aunt Hilda and Uncle Ethan and Hans were coming to our house. Of course Elsie and Jed were invited. Also Jed's parents and his brother, Will. If we could get Papa into a good mood Thanksgiving would be a lot of fun for everyone. Elsie hadn't wanted to come at first, but Mama told her she had to make peace with Papa sooner or later and it might as well be sooner.

166

Now I wondered just how peaceful Papa was going to be when Mama told him about all she had done today. I was glad it was too late for him to do anything to change it.

Vina and I did the dishes. We wanted to stay close by to hear what Papa said when she told him. But as soon as the last pan was dried and put away Mama said, "Lucy, you and Mae go on to bed. Papa and I and the older girls have some talking to do." They went without a murmur. Vina and I looked at each other. Why us? Did Mama think Papa would hold his temper if we were there?

"Sam, I've some news for you and I've asked the girls to stay and hear it because it concerns their future too, and they are old enough to share in such things."

Papa looked up from his paper. "What have you been up to now?"

"Quite a lot, as you'll soon know. Sit down, girls."

Gathered around the kitchen table Mama told the whole story. Why she hadn't mailed Papa's letter to Uncle Phil; about her visit to Close Real Estate Company two weeks ago and the letter she had received yesterday. Then she mentioned the trip to town today and what she had done, with Mr. Plover's and the bank's advice. Papa sat very still, looking down at the table. He didn't interrupt or lift his eyes while Mama was telling all this.

"I couldn't discuss any of it with you, Sam. You haven't been yourself lately, not since Spaulding did what he did. But neither could I sit back and let you lose everything we've all worked so hard to build here in Iowa. Our life is here now, Sam. Not in Saunemin. When I bought that farm back it was not my idea to return there. It was an investment for the money papa left me. Now we needed to sell it again in order to keep this farm. When I asked Mr. Close to find a buyer, that was all I had in mind. But when I saw Mr. Close today to sign the deed and accept the money, he suggested what I finally did." She stopped to get her breath.

Papa asked me to bring him a cup of coffee if there was any, but made no other comment. He sipped it slowly still staring at the table.

"Both Mr. Close, and Mr. Plover later, explained that by putting the money I received for the Saunemin farm into income property, we could take care of the hardware debts and reopen the store and have enough reserve capital to carry us until next year's crops are harvested. The bank has agreed to renew the present mortgage on this farm, which will give you a chance to pay it off out of farm earnings. I'm sure father would approve of the use I have made of the money left to me, and I hope you will too, Sam."

For several minutes Papa just sat there staring at the table. Then he got up slowly, put on his jacket and cap and went out.

"What's he going to do, Mama?" I asked.

"Nothing for you girls to worry about. Your father just needs time to digest all the news." She smiled. "It *was* a pretty big mouthful, wasn't it? But he'll be all right. Now you'd better go on to bed. I'll wait up for him."

We went to bed, but not to sleep. There was too much to talk about. Vina was as excited about Mama owning those stores as I was. "Will we be rich now?" she asked in an awed whisper.

"I don't know. I haven't had time to think about it." And this was true. I'd been more concerned about not having to move away. Now I thought about Vina's question. It would be nice to be rich enough to live in a big house with fine furniture and have all the pretty dresses we wanted. And enough money to visit Grandma every year, and maybe when we were older, see the big cities. But right now there were so many thing to be happy about how could I tell whether I'd be any happier if we were rich?

I didn't know Papa had come in until I heard his voice in the kitchen.

"All right, Molly. What's done is done. I'm not saying it was the best thing to do but there's no turning back now. We've got to live with it whatever happens."

"Did you really want to turn back, Sam? Give up all we have here?" Papa didn't answer. Mama said, "No, I'm sure you didn't. And thank God we don't have to."

"God and Father Dauber! You're forgetting it was *his* money."

Mama laughed. "All right, Sam! But I think God had a good deal to do with Papa having the money to leave to me."

The kitchen was quiet for a while. Then Papa asked, "Now

that you've got the hardware store out of hock, who's going to run it? I sure can't and look after the farm too."

"Time enough to decide that. There's the legal work still to be done. And when we do reopen the store, maybe we should do it in some special way."

"Was that Plover's idea or yours?"

"Mine, I guess. I haven't mentioned it to Mr. Plover."

"Sometimes, Molly Bullard, I wonder who's wearing the pants in this family, you or me!"

Vina giggled. We could go to sleep now. Peace had been restored.

Thanksgiving Day was a real celebration that year. It was hard to believe that so short a time ago I had looked forward to it with dread. Papa was jovial all through dinner. In spite of the terrible things he had said about God that night when he argued with Mama over money, I think he was really thankful for all that had happened to make this day festive. Peace between Elsie and him was restored without harsh words. He treated her now as the grownup she was, with a husband to tell her what to do or not to do, if telling was needed.

After dinner, Papa made a fire in the base-burner in the parlor. As soon as we were all comfortable — except for being too full — he announced that the hardware store would be opened next week. "Just in time for Christmas business, let me remind you! Also, the store will have a new name, *Bullard Hardware*."

Uncle Ethan glanced at Mama before he said, "Why, that's great, Sam! Just great!"

Papa leaned back in his special chair. "Never should have gone into business with a man like Spaulding. I should have known he'd run out the minute he got us into trouble. A man has to stand up to his problems, lick them before they lick him."

"That's sure right, Sam," Mr. Miller said. "This new country is no place for weaklings or cowards. Now you take the time that city feller . . ."

I was ready to burst, I was so mad! *How* could Papa sit there and say such things? He'd been more than willing to run.

169

Any place — back to Saunemin or some new place — rather than face the people he owed money. And he would have run, too, if Mama hadn't stoppd him. Now he acted like it was *his doing!* Making Mr. Miller believe that. Elsie knew it wasn't true. I could tell by the way she looked at Mama and grinned. But why didn't Mama *say* something? Was this her way of helping Papa keep his pioneering spirit? Did she have to let him take all the credit? It didn't seem fair! I was surprised he hadn't claimed *he* purchased the new buildings, too.

I felt sure Uncle Ethan knew all about the new buildings; that Mama had talked with him before she went to see Mr. Close in the first place. As for us girls, we knew all of this was family business and not to be talked about at school or church or elsewhere.

The hardware store was reopened, bearing a big new sign: BULLARD HARDWARE. It was a big affair, with souvenirs, root-beer, coffee and popcorn for everyone. Vina and I had spent the whole day Friday popping corn until we had a washtub full. Opening Day was Saturday. Fortunately the sky was clear even though the wind was pretty cold. Mama and Papa were busy greeting customers. Vina and I dished up popcorn and served beverages. Most of the older people gathered around the stove as soon as they arrived, warming their fingers on a tincup of hot coffee. Papa strutted about like a proud rooster, greeting the men with a hearty handshake and sometimes a slap on the back. Mama greeted the women and saw that each had a souvenir. There were rubber balloons for the children.

Today Papa's pioneering spirit had really come to life!

Later, on the way home, Mama said it had been a good day, financially and in many other ways. And now I understood why she had let Papa take all the credit. From her conversation with Papa I learned that *she* owned the hardware store and the two buildings. Not Papa. Mr. Plover had made that clear in the papers he had drawn up. Mama alone had signed them.

Papa grumbled about this on the way home. "What's yours is mine," he again insisted.

Mama said firmly, "No, Sam. Not this time. These are *my* investments."

Strangely, Papa didn't make a fuss about it. He seemed satisfied that his name was on the sign and that he got credit for being a smart businessman. I think what pleased him most was that he now considered himself a real pioneer.

But it was Mama who managed things, and approved credit only when she decided it was safe and right.

Each morning now, as soon as the chores were done, Papa drove to town. Usually he dropped Vina and Lucy and me off at the schoolhouse on the way, and unless the snow was too deep we walked home. Often we got a ride with one of the neighbors. However we got home, there were the chores awaiting us. Papa never came home in time to help with them. He seemed to have forgotten his declaration the night Mama told him about getting the hardware store back; that he wouldn't have time to run it. He had done little else since the opening day. We girls thought it was awfully unfair that we had to wade through snow day after day doing a man's work, while Papa was sitting in a warm store swaping stories with the customers. Why didn't Mama run the store and let Papa take care of the farm?

When we asked her this question she said, "It's best this way for now, dear."

At supper each night we listened to his reports of the day's events. How farmers came to the store asking his advice on some problem, or an investment. I noticed that Mama listened politely with that little smile about her lips which told me she was thinking secret thoughts. And as soon as supper was over and Papa was through bragging, she would ask him for the day's business records and they would go over these together. *She* decided the purchases to be made, and when credit was to be extended or had reached its limit. Often there were arguments, but somehow Mama managed to make him see things her way without making him angry. Letting Papa take credit which she might deserve was her way of helping him get back his self-respect and pioneering spirit. These, she had told me, were more important than praise.

Only much later I realized how greatly our lives also were being changed and given purposeful direction.

With spring on the way, Mama said, "Sam, we're going to have to hire somebody to do the plowing and planting, or to run the store while you do it."

Papa agreed. "But I don't know where in thunderation I'm

171

going to find anyone I can trust with either job. Couldn't you look after the store while I get the crops in?"

"I could, but who would do the cooking and washing and baking?"

"The kids can do that. They're old enough and it's time they learned."

"Not and keep up with their school work."

"It won't hurt them to miss a few weeks of school. They're more ways to learn than from books."

"Don't you think they have had more than their share of that kind of education, Sam? They are *girls!* Isn't it about time you started treating them that way, stopped expecting them to do a man's work?"

Papa just looked at her crossly for a minute. "All right, Molly. You're running this shebang now, not me. Do what you want to about the spring work."

The next morning at breakfast Mama told him she thought it might be easier to find someone to look after the store than to do the farm work. "Everyone capable of doing our plowing and planting has his own to do. Perhaps Mr. Bruckner or Mr. Plover can recommend someone, unless you have someone in mind."

"I don't. And *you'd* better talk to Bruckner and Plover. They're more likely to put themselves out for you."

"You know that's not true, Sam." But she went to town with Papa that morning.

Mr. Plover suggested Donald Matthews. The Matthews had recently moved to Stebbinsville from Davenport, and Dr. Matthews had opened an office in the same building. Donald, he said, had worked in a general store in Davenport while finishing school, and was looking for something to do to help out until his father's practice increased. Mama hired him. She explained about the accounts and that she would go over them each week with him. Papa gave him instructions about selling, although Donald probably knew as much about that as Papa did if he had worked in a Davenport store.

Papa seemed glad to be back doing farm work. Especially now that the weather was nice. Uncle Ethan and Jed helped him in their spare time. We girls now did only the morning

172

milking. Mama spent more time helping Elsie, so Vina and I did most of the housework.

"Why can't Elsie do her own work?" Vina asked.

"Because she's going to have a baby, that's why!"

Vina's eyes popped. She knew a lot more about such things than I did at her age. She'd been around the barn and corrals enough to figure things out for herself. "Isn't Elsie *afraid?*"

"I don't think so. Mama says Elsie's very happy and Jed's so proud he can't wait for it to get here. He's sure it will be a boy."

"Well, *I'd* be scared. A baby's nice, but I don't see why you have to be sick to have one."

That year brought other excitement into our lives. Sometimes it seemed too much was happening at once. There was scarcely time to be excited about one event before something else happened. The church we had waited for at last was being built. The fund, started by a pie supper, was now big enough to pay for the building and provide a minister. There had been many socials and benefits during the past two years, and donations from most of the farmers in the community. As soon as crops were planted, the church building began. And the Board began to look around for a proper minister. Finally they agreed to accept Rev. Martin Pritchard, just graduated from the Seminary. Our church would be his first pastorate.

Mr. Miller made the announcement at Bible Study meeting. "All of us agreed a young minister would be most suitable. A man who could grow with our community. We hope all of you will approve our selection. Rev. Pritchard will be here in time to conduct services in our new church next Sunday. I know everyone will want to be there to welcome him."

Where the minister would live was then discussed. It would be a while, Mr. Miller said, before a parsonage could be built. Mr. Evans offered to share his house with Reverend Pritchard for as long as necessary.

During the next week while the pews and pulpit were being installed, and everything made ready for Sunday, the community buzzed with anticipation. The older girls at school talked of little else. A young preacher, they whispered, *had* to be handsome. And he must be unmarried. Mr. Miller hadn't said anything about a Mrs. Pritchard.

173

Rev. Pritchard arrived on Friday. Literary Society was meeting that night in the schoolhouse, and of course Mr. Evans would bring him. There was sure to be a big crowd, Mama said. "More curiosity, I'm afraid, than interest in recitations and entertainment," she predicted, smiling.

"Can't blame 'em," Papa said. "Quite a few unmarried girls old enough to be interested. I don't envy Pritchard. He's going to be in for a rough time."

It certainly looked that way when we arrived at the schoolhouse Friday night. The room was so crowded Papa had to make a path for us to get inside. In the center of the room, almost surrounded by women and girls, were Mr. Evans and a tall young man. He *was* handsome, as the girls at school had assumed, but I thought he looked a little frightened by so much attention. Mr. Evans saw us and brought Rev. Pritchard to meet Mama and Papa.

"Mrs. Bullard, more than any of us, is responsible for our having a church," he said warmly. "Without her determination I'm afraid we'd still be using the schoolhouse for Sunday meetings."

Mama thanked him. "Mr. Evans gives me far too much credit," she said, shaking hands with Rev. Pritchard. "Everyone has worked very hard for the church. It's a great pleasure to have you here to help us make it meaningful." She turned to us. "These are our daughters, Ann and Alvina."

Rev. Pritchard bowed. "Delighted, Miss Ann and Miss Alvina." I said thank-you. Vina just blushed.

All evening the women and girls, and some of the men, went on making a fuss over the new minister. He was taller than Papa, with thick brown hair and grey eyes that seemed to light up when he spoke to you. He made you feel he was listening to what you were saying and thought it important, Mama told Papa when we were finally seated.

"Seems sincere all right," Papa agreed, "but he might be a little *too* young and handsome. You can't expect much in the way of a sermon from a man just out of the Seminary."

"Let's wait and see," Mama replied.

Sunday was a beautiful spring day. It was as if God was smiling down on our new church and minister, I thought. Families came from every corner of our growing community, dressed in their best. In the bright sunlight the church glistened with its coat of white paint and tall steeple. Inside, every pew was filled. When the congregation rose to sing *Praise God From Whom All Blessing Flow,* no one could doubt that the song came from their hearts.

A hush fell over the room as Rev Pritchard took his place behind the pulpit. In clear reverent voice he read, "*Except the Lord build the house, they labor in vain that build it; except the Lord keep the city, the watchman waketh but in vain.*" His prayer was softly spoken as if he knew he had only to ask and God would hear him. His sermon was one to remember. Even Papa commented on the way home, "He may be young, Molly, but by golly he sure can preach!"

The story of Ann and her family are continued in the sequel to **This Rough New Land.** The Bullard girls become young women and encounter romance, hard times and tragedy in volume two of Sunrise Books' **Ann of the Prairie** series, available at your local bookstore or from the publisher.

A WORD FROM
THE PUBLISHER

We at Sunrise Books have a special commitment to you, the reader, in offering you a quality, wholesome book.

If this book has been such for you, we would encourage you to try another Sunrise Book. Your local bookstore is the first place to check for all your book needs. If they are unable to help you, or if there's not a bookstore convenient for you, we would be proud to serve you.

Sunrise Books
1707 E Street
Eureka, CA 95501
(707) 442-4004, ext. 23